# Wild Trails
# Wild Tales

# Wild Trails
# Wild Tales

*Bernard McKay*

*illustrated by*

*Wendy Liddle*

hancock

house

ISBN 0-88839-395-4
Copyright © 1996 Bernard McKay

Second printing 2000

---

**Cataloging in Publication Data**
McKay, Bernard
    Wild trails, wild tales

    ISBN 0-88839-395-4

    1. McKay, Bernard. 2. Hunting guides--British Columbia--
    Biography. 3. Trappers--British Columbia--Biography.
    4. Outdoor life--British Columbia--Anecdotes.
    I. Liddle, Wendy. II. Title.
    SK152.B7M34 1996        799.292        C96-910394-8

---

Printed in Canada—Kromar

Production: Nancy Miller and Myron Shutty
Editing: Karen Kloeble
Cover photos: Bernard McKay


Published simultaneously in Canada and the United States by

**HANCOCK HOUSE PUBLISHERS LTD.**
19313 Zero Avenue, Surrey, B.C. V4P 1M7

**HANCOCK HOUSE PUBLISHERS**
1431 Harrison Avenue, Blaine, WA 98230-5005

(604) 538-1114    Fax (604) 538-2262
(800) 938-1114    Fax (800) 983-2262
*Web Site:* www.hancockhouse.com   *email:* sales@hancockhouse.com

# Contents

# Foreword

Bernard McKay is one of the few remaining people who truly makes his living from the land. By profession, he's a trapper, a guide and outfitter, but he does just about anything he puts his mind to, and he does it well. Part of the secret to his success are his observational skills. Bernard not only looks, he also sees. Then he thinks about what he saw and what it might mean.

Like most rural people, Bernard has stories to tell of when things went right and when they didn't. Because of the extent of his experience, his stories span thousands of square miles and decades of time. This book contains but a few of those stories.

Bernard decided early that he wanted to work and live beyond the end of the pavement and he's achieved his goal through an immense amount of unabated effort. Not only that, he's found a wonderful woman, Jo-Eane, to share his life. They've raised six children, all of whom share their appreciation of the wilds of British Columbia from their home on Hoodoo Lake.

It has been my pleasure to help Bernard compile his stories. As a wildlife ecologist, I've been pleasantly surprised by the accuracy of Bernie's observations. While I've explained some minor points of animal behavior to him, I've not needed to explain much. This is one man who has obviously given a lot of thought to what he's seen and done. The words are his, the subjects and experiences they relate are his and I hope the enjoyment of them will be as much yours as it was mine.

Warren G. Eastland
Ph.D. Wildlife Ecologist

# Introduction

For as long as I can remember I've loved the outdoors. My mother still reminds me that when people asked me what I wanted to be when I grew up I would say, "a hermit in the bush." As a lad of twelve, I would spend hours in the bush behind our small farm near Langley, B.C. Soon, I had rounded up a few old rusty traps and began to thin out the skunks and civet cats around the area. By fourteen years of age, I had a .22 and an old double-barrel shotgun. I hunted ring-necked pheasants, numerous in the area at that time, and even got one red fox.

I let the word out that I was interested in any deer hides and practiced skinning and tanning these, along with possums and raccoons that were given to me. I skinned out the dogs and cats that had been road-killed and even made a few garments out of the hides. My cat skin belt drew a few guffaws when I wore it one day to junior high school. Once, after skinning out a skunk, (it was first necessary to bury it for three days to kill most of the smell) I was a little whiffy so I had a good shower before going to school. I thought I smelled okay but, as the grade nine classroom warmed up, even I noticed the peculiar odor that was rising around me. A few of the girls were moving away from me to vacant desks at the back of the classroom. The teacher said it might be best if I went home early that day.

When I was fifteen and sixteen years old, I cajoled my way into a few real hunting trips with some deer hunting men around our area. One fall I traveled to the Yalakom River near Lillooet with an old family friend, Bill Shetterly, his son Lane and my Dad. Although we didn't get anything on this trip I had a terrific time and I was hooked for life on hunting.

Like most young men, I got a little sidetracked in my late teens with cars and girls. When I married, however, I took up where I left off, making the trip to Prince George each fall to hunt for moose. By now I had a truck and camper and most weekends in the summer saw my wife, Jo-Eane, and I going fishing somewhere in the interior. In 1972, we moved just north of Prince George and it was the best move a young man could have made. There was lots of work then and I got a job in a tire shop right away. We were at the center of great fishing and hunting country. By 1976, we moved to our present location at Hoodoo Lake, thirty miles northwest of town.

I began trapping around 1976 and soon had my own registered trapline. This was also the start of my guiding career. Through the 1980s, I worked as an assistant big game guide for many outfitters across the north. It was here that I garnered the experience and savvy I needed to own my own guiding business one day. In 1990, my brother Pat and I went into partnership and purchased the guiding rights to a 900 square-mile area just north of Prince George. We are operating it still. My short stories tell some of the adventures I've been fortunate enough to experience over the years. I've enjoyed writing this book as it has brought back many good memories. I hope these true accounts will stir the readers' sense of adventure.

# Deadly Errors

Now and then the beasts of the bush commit an error in judgment that has tragic results.

At first it sounded like two trees moaning as they rubbed together in the wind, but the air was still this fall morning. I carried on walking, quietly watching the lake shore for moose. This time the sound was close and I knew it wasn't trees. It took a few minutes to locate but the third low moan did it. Just ahead, in a jack pine, was a large black bear cub looking down at me. Instinctively, I slid my thumb up and flicked off the safety on my .270 as I searched for the sow that should be close by. I didn't want a bear, especially a sow with a cub, so I moved away slowly, watching in all directions as I went.

I sat on a log, well back from the cub, which afforded a good view all around. The cub slowly descended the tree and walked over a small knoll and out of sight. Still no sign of the mother. I stood up and could see the cub on top of a black log. The youngster just laid there and looked back at me. After twenty minutes, certain there was no other bear around, I went over for a better look at what the cub was doing. The black log was a dead bear—the sow! As I approached, the cub again went up a tree.

The mother bear had gone to the lake shore by going down the steep bank that was covered by thick willows. Unbeknownst to her, there was a four-inch thick dry snag, pointed like a spear, faced at an angle up the hill. She must have half-slid down the hill and impaled herself on that snag. The spear took her below the chin and went into her lower neck and chest. It was a one in a thousand weird accident.

The mountain goat is a surefooted animal—he has to be. The cliffs the goat calls home have no patience for clumsiness. A friend and fellow big game guide related the following story that took place some years ago in the Spatsizi Park area of B.C.

Two guides and two hunters watched from camp as an old nanny goat led a troop of mountain goats down what looked like from below to be a sheer cliff face. The goats were following a narrow ledge that traversed the cliff. The ledge stopped right above another ledge that carried on. The nanny leaped down to this new ledge and one by one the other eight followed her example. This new ledge petered out to nothing after fifty feet. The goats turned around but discovered they could not make the leap back up to the original ledge.

The goats, seemingly unconcerned, bedded down on the narrow ledge as best they could. Five hours later the goats were getting restless. First one goat unsuccessfully tried to pull himself up with his front legs. Then he made a desperate jump up but tumbled backward to his death. Goat number two gave it a try. He too dropped to his doom. That left seven on the cliff. Just before dark another goat fell off.

The next morning only three remained in sight. By noon, another had fallen off in full view of the men. The last two goats were still there when darkness returned. In the morning all the goats were gone. The men hiked over to the base of the cliff where all nine goats lay dead on the rocks.

There is very little room for error in the animal kingdom. Mistakes usually result in death or injury; that's nature's way.

# Wolf

I could hear them howling a long way off; they had to be a mile up river.

It was 2:00 A.M. and I was sleeping under the stars with giant spruce trees for bedposts. I had never had any trouble with wolves in the past. The pack was getting closer now and howling steady as they traveled. It was May and I was beaver trapping. Several carcasses were laying by the edge of the river a few feet away from me. I wonder if the wolves will smell them, I thought.

The wolves were now less than one hundred yards away and on my side of the river. My rifle was leaning against a tree near my head. I moved it down beside my sleeping bag in case I knocked it over. I didn't want to damage the scope. Where was my flashlight? Better dig it out so it is handy, just in case I have to get up to stoke the fire or something. Looks like the fire's out though.

The horned owl that's been whoo-whooing since dark has now shut up. The wolves are now silent. For some reason, I'm wide awake. I remember reading about two loggers up in Fort Nelson who had to kill a wolf that attacked them two years back. There was also a trapper near Williams Lake who, like me, was camping out in a sleeping bag when a wolf bit him on the hip and drew blood right through the bag. A rancher, thinking it must be rabid, shot the wolf. Tests showed it wasn't. I've heard the Carrier Indians tell stories of the days before firearms when wolf packs would raid the villages killing children and carrying them off. I'm not worried though. The experts today say there's never been a case of wolves attacking men.

I can hear the pack as it circles my camp, the odd twig breaking, bush moving. Darn it, where's the moon when you need it? That spruce is lousy wood and sure burns out fast, not a flicker left of that campfire. Everything is dead silent now except for the gurgling of the river; it's not worried by a few wolves. Then it happened. The howling started again. The wolves had passed me and were again headed down river. I wasn't worried for a minute.

# Dangerous River

In 1993, three of us—my son Jason, a friend Rod Thiessen and I—went on a hunt to the Halfway River north of Hudson Hope near the Peace River country. We had along a big tent and had planned to hunt the seismic trails for moose and deer.

After three days of walking and scouting the country, we were still without meat to bring home. I could see on my map that the Graham River flowed through some remote country before entering the Halfway and there appeared to be a ranch road to the river's upper reaches. After some discussion we decided to take my nineteen-foot freight canoe and drift down this river. The fifty-mile trip normally should take about three days allowing time for hunting. I talked to a few of the ranchers in the area, but none of them seemed to know what the river was like.

It was calm where we launched our canoe, deceptively calm, but around the first bend the river accelerated as it went over a rock garden. The upper third of the river was almost continuously like this and we had little time to sightsee. I was busy with my pole at the stern and the other two men were helping me steer clear of the rocks; even so, we bumped over many that were just under the surface. I had put Teflon on the bottom of the boat and this extra protection saved the hull considerably.

When we had time to look around, the country was beautiful. By noon of that first day we were entering mountainous country with the river sweeping in great arcs across the valley floor. An old burn surrounded us and it looked like a good game area. We saw the tracks of elk, moose and deer on the sand bars but never the authors of the tracks. We camped in a scenic spot that afternoon and I tried to call for moose but had no takers.

In the morning we were again working hard on the swift river. We had just come through a fast stretch and into calmer water when a buck deer ran out onto the beach. In one smooth motion, Rod raised his rifle and fired. The deer spun around and ran into the willows. I beached the canoe and after a short search we found the animal 100 feet back from the river. It was only a spike buck (two years old with unbranched antlers) and would be good to eat.

With light hearts we were soon on our way again. About an hour later I noticed the current speeding up. The river began to funnel into chutes but we rose to the occasion each time and had confidence in our ability to handle anything this river could throw at us. Alas, pride goeth before a fall.

We came to a point where the Graham River was cutting itself down to the level of the Halfway River. To do this it thundered down through a canyon. It was difficult running the beginning of this canyon through the boulders and high waves, places where we should have lined the boat down slowly from

shore. We came to a place where there was no turning back. Over a lip we went at breakneck speed and down a 200-foot chute through a maze of boulders. At the bottom of the long chute we could not turn the canoe fast enough to squeeze through the only passage available. The canoe rode up on a rock, partially flipped on its side in the rushing rapids and jammed between two boulders. Instantly the boat filled with water. Jason and Rod managed to scramble up on a rock while I stayed with the boat. The two men still had the presence of mind to hang onto the bow line. This prevented the canoe from going under completely, where it no doubt would have broken its back.

I worked in the stern to salvage the sleeping bags and the gear that had not been washed away. I heaved the deer up onto the boulders and threw the bags and rifles to the men. We then slowly pulled the boat to higher ground. The remainder of our trip was taken with considerably more caution. We lined the boat past the worst of the rapids until we were clear of the canyon. That night I had to sleep beside the campfire to stay warm as my sleeping bag was soaked.

Day three saw us reach the Halfway River and the end of our trip. My boat had several broken ribs and my camera was shot. We had lost a paddle and a bit of our pride, but still had our hides intact. It will likely be some time before we ever run the Graham River again.

# On the Trapline

Trapping is a way of life that is over 400 years old. The trapping of wild fur is what established our country. Indeed, right up to the 1800s it was almost the only industry in Canada. Trapping has changed dramatically since I started in the mid-1970s. Then, the leg-hold trap was the most common trap in use. Today (1996) it is rarely used. In fact, it is banned by law for all animals except the wolf, coyote and lynx; even here the jaws must be padded by rubber so as not to cut the skin or break bones. A body-grabbing or quick-kill trap, like the conibear, is what the modern trappers all use. The snowmobile, used extensively, has enabled the trapper to cover more country and check his traps more often. Snowshoes are still a necessity in the rough country. Over 3,000 trappers still get all or part of their annual income from trapping in British Columbia. The annual catch has been stable for many years, suggesting trappers are working their areas wisely.

The weather was getting colder this snowy November day. I could hear the river ice booming and cracking as I slept in my little line shack at the junction of the Salmon and Muskeg Rivers, about fifty miles northwest of Prince George. I had come in by snowmobile to this point the day before, checking my traps as I went. November 21. The season was only three weeks old and I had caught about twenty martens, a few minks, three otters, two coyotes, numerous beaver and muskrats, and the usual assortment of squirrels and weasels. Tomorrow I would head up river.

Morning came and I rustled up some pancakes and bacon for myself and then stepped outside to start the day. I was glad to leave the noisy snowmobile behind; today I would be pulling my six-foot toboggan. At times the snowmobile is a curse, as you're getting stuck all the time in deep snow and lake slush. Pulling on 350 pounds of sled until your back is sore is an everyday occurrence.

17

My tump line forehead leather was partially frozen, so I warmed it under my coat for a few minutes. I've found the tump line is the best way to pull a toboggan behind you because it leaves your hands free to carry a rifle or ax. My trail wound through the willow for a ways then left the river to follow a spruce-covered ridge. Here were my first traps and I had something—a whiskey jack. Now there's no money in birds, so I reset the trap and placed fresh bait right at the back of the marten box. I have covered the back of the box with a screen so the birds (whiskey jacks, Steller's jays and chickadees) can feed without any danger to themselves. However, there are always a few impatient ones that try to go inside and the consequences are fatal.

A quarter of a mile further and this time I have a big male marten and a white weasel (or ermine), one in each trap. I'm using the newest 120-magnum conibear trap here. These have been tested and are designed to kill the animal instantly and by the looks of the marten he never moved. These new traps break the animal's neck and they will break your thumb, too, if you're not careful when resetting them.

There is about eighteen inches of snow on the ground and all the trees are heavily covered. It is a silent world as I slowly snowshoe along my path. Two whiskey jacks come out of nowhere and begin to follow me. No doubt they spot the red beaver meat on my sleigh. It's nice to have their company and I stop for a rest and dig out a piece of meat for them. Occasionally, I hear a woodpecker hammering on a dry snag, probably a mile up the river.

I'm now back at the river; this is where I cross to the other side. I have a pair of hip waders hanging from a branch and I put these on. Most of the river is frozen right across but the ice is not yet thick enough to support a man, so I cross where the water is open at a small rapid. It should be only eighteen inches deep here; it's not. The river has risen considerably with the fresh snowfalls we have had and the water looks too deep for my waders. I strip all my clothes off from the waist down and put on the waders. Holding my toboggan shoulder-high I step in and in a few steps I'm over the tops of the boots. The water is almost

waist deep and about one-inch cold; luckily I have only a short distance to go to reach the far shore. The raven watching me must be having a good laugh at this sight. After rubbing some life back into my legs and putting on my dry clothes I'm off again.

At first I'm not sure what it is that's coming toward me. I stop, and down the trail comes a snowshoe hare hopping very slowly. I'm sure he can see me, but he continues until he stops about a foot away from my boot and looks at me. This is definitely strange behavior for a normally shy animal. Thirty feet behind the hare I see a marten coming my way; he stops on the trail, I pull my .22 out of my backpack and approach the marten. He has just enough energy left to climb up a small balsam tree. One shot and the marten is mine and the rabbit carries on—his lucky day. That desperate chase must have been going on for many miles as both animals were all in.

Three miles and two more martens later, my small cabin comes into sight. I've traveled about five miles since this morning. Seven miles is a very full day for a trapper on foot; he's weighed down with a backpack, heavy clothes, snowshoes, rifle and a sleigh with forty pounds of bait and traps. I light the cabin heater and make a pot of tea. After lunch I'm off again up river to check a wolverine set I have made, as well as some snares I've placed to catch coyotes. I'll be back before dark.

The wolverine has not been around; last week I saw where he had crossed the river several times. This animal is a tireless traveler and may cover fifty miles before swinging back my way. My snares are also bereft of any coyotes; I keep on.

He just sat there on his hind haunches, patiently looking at me as I approached—a big tom lynx! I didn't expect this in a marten trap! The old cat had put his paw into the marten box and the little marten trap had him by two toes. I dispatched him with my rifle and walked over to inspect him. He was a beautiful animal and the pelt was in prime shape. I was lighthearted as I headed back to my still warm cabin. This lynx would bring me $150 on the sale, double that if I tanned it and sold it to one of my hunters next fall.

A trapper's day is short in midwinter. It is almost 8:00 A.M. before there's enough light to travel. Around 3:30 P.M., the shadows are getting long and it is time to be getting back to the old cabin. In the long evenings I play a lot of solitaire, read by candlelight, or just lay back on the bunk watching the flicker from the fire on the ceiling while I rest sore muscles for the next day. You have to enjoy your own company in this business.

In the morning I start back, retracing my steps from the day before, including my polar bear dip in the river. I pick up another marten and a few squirrels that have come to get the beaver meat bait. Most people are unaware that squirrels are meat eaters. In the spring, they kill and eat baby robins right out of the nest. I notice the moose are beginning to work over the willow flats along the river. The wolves won't be far behind, so I set a snare for them right on my trail.

Three days from now I'll repeat the process again. The river should be frozen solid by then as the temperature is dropping. My story is not unique. It is acted out across the north by thousands of trappers plying their lonely trade and enjoying the wilderness around them.

# Some Bears Don't Sleep

Bears, black and grizzly, hibernate in winter; everyone knows that and all the books on bears will attest to the fact. I've run into bears that haven't read those books, I guess. For a trapper there is only one thing more dangerous than thin ice and that's a bear who is still out and about in early winter.

When mishap or death of a sow bear results in an orphaned cub, the young animal has no one to teach it the skills of building a winter den. The cub must have a feeling for hibernating but is not sure what to do. He may just lay under a couple of dead falls and be driven out by the first good freezing rain of late fall. It was just such a bear that was giving me headaches one winter.

As I made my rounds checking my marten and lynx traps, the tracks of a small black bear appeared on the trail. I arrived at every trap location for the next few miles to find the bait gone and the trap sprung. This bear had stumbled into my area and had found himself a nice bread line. He ate the beaver meat I used and broke up all my cubbies (these are small tepee shaped huts that I build for the trapping of lynx). It took three weeks for this pest to finally go to bed and leave me alone for the rest of the winter.

Of far more concern for the trapper is the grizzly bear. Some of these bears are very late going into hibernation and may roam the snowy woods until mid-December. A large male grizzly surprised an Indian trapper near Ft. St. John one winter. The man had lost a lot of fur to the bear and was attempting to track the beast down. The story was pieced together by the RCMP using the clear sign left in the snow. It was a classic case of the hunter becoming the hunted. The grizzly is a cunning animal if he knows he is being followed. This animal circled and came up from behind using the soft snow to hide the sound of his approach. The man was found lying face down in the snow with his skull crushed. The authorities killed the culprit later and its front paw measured nine inches across!

I was getting jumpy. I had seen the grizzly in the summer walking the lakeshore. It was a big blond specimen and now I could see it circling me in the pines. "December 10, what's he still doing out?" I thought. I had been checking traps along the shore of Raccoon Lake and in four locations the bear had been there before me. He had eaten the bait, smashed the marten boxes off the trees and even eaten a mink that was in a trap. I was about a half-mile from my snowmobile and safety. The snow was only a foot deep so I had not bothered with snowshoes when I walked to this last trap set. I was armed with a popgun, for grizzly anyway, a .22 single shot. I knew better than to run, as I've often seen how fast a bear can move. I started walking backwards toward the lake, keeping my eyes on the bear. The bear began walking parallel to me and only watching me out of the corner of his eyes. I traveled in this fashion for a ways, bumping into trees and trying not to fall over as that could trigger an attack. When the bear disappeared behind some blow-down I turned and ran like hell. I didn't look back until I was on the machine and going 40 mph down the lake; normally my machine will only do thirty. I never saw that bear again.

The year was 1948. Two men walked over 100 miles north of Kispiox, B.C. into their trapline on the Upper Skeena River. They had with them all their supplies for the winter. They packed six dogs using saddlebag-type dog packs and carried the rest on their own backs. They arrived at their cabin as the first snows of winter began to fall, and it falls deep in that country. By mid-December the snow lay deep and the brothers were busy with their work: trapping, snowshoeing long miles each day, skinning out their catch by candlelight at night and stretching and drying the fur. The dogs were tied up most of the time as they didn't use them much on their rounds. Late one afternoon, as the men were slogging back to the cabin, they noticed the tracks of a grizzly bear on the trail. The tracks were headed for the cabin as well. With foreboding, the men silently and carefully made their way back. As they approached the cabin, they could see five dogs still tied up; one was gone. The dogs were quiet so the men knew the bear was no longer around. The cabin was a shambles: their side of bacon gone, flour and rice spread about the floor and everything knocked off the shelves. The fur catch was safely up a tree in a cache so it was all right.

In the morning the men armed themselves and started down the path the grizzly had taken. The missing dog must have managed to break his leash and they could see where he had followed the bear. Only ten minutes out of camp there was the dog, or what was left of him. Now, usually a dog is agile enough to stay out of a bear's reach. The spoor in the snow showed where the bear had lain behind a large spruce tree waiting for the dog. The dog never made it past the tree. The bear hit the dog a tremendous blow and the dog's head was driven back between its shoulder blades, with the shoulders split apart. The two men had a sobering walk back to camp that afternoon. The grizzly never again bothered the trappers and must have left the country.

23

# Not Too Old

I received the letter in the summer of 1990. Two mature hunters and their wives would be coming up from the U.S. to hunt for moose in the fall. When I talked to Sid and his partner Del they told me they had been hunting partners for fifty years. "Just how old are you boys?" I asked. It turns out Sid was seventy-nine and Del eighty-one years old. Using all the tact I could think of, I felt them out as to their ability to still get around in the bush. They assured me everything would be fine.

My brother (and partner) Pat and I were a little apprehensive as the two hunters pulled into our yard at Hoodoo Lake. These would be the oldest hunters either of us had ever guided. Sid no sooner got out of his truck than he had to show me his "punk medicine," a short-barreled shotgun mounted on the floor in front of his seat. "This baby keeps the bikers and other punks from hassling us when we're out on the highway," Sid said. Del was just as spunky and he threw his heavy duffle around with ease. I looked at Pat and we both were thinking the same thing—these guys are characters.

It was at the breakfast table that I first noticed it. Sid had Parkinson's disease and at times his hands shook badly; in fact, his wife would steady them for him as he ate. "How's your shooting, Sid?" I asked. "You just show me a moose," he said, "and I'll do my part."

Pat took the two hunters out that day, but saw nothing. When they returned they looked tired but had handled the day's short hike just fine. "Tomorrow we'll be going to one of our horse camps," Pat told them. "We won't have to ride a horse will we?" asked Del. Pat assured them they could walk in the two miles.

When the three men reached the camp and lake, the two old fellows had a short nap while Pat scouted around. About 4:00 P.M., they headed out in the boat to look for moose on the swampy lake. Just before dark, a bull and cow stepped from shore and stood in ankle deep water. Pat rowed the boat as close as he dared and Del shot. Down went the cow in two feet of water, but the bull bolted for the timber before Sid could shoot. Now the work began.

Pat had been standing in the water for twenty minutes, with the old timers helping the best they could, when the three of them looked up at a splashing sound. The bull was back to look for his girl friend! Sid raised his rifle to take aim. His hands were shaking badly and so was the rifle. After a few seconds he took a deep breath and held it, the hands steadied for a split second and that was all it took. Down went the bull—a good clean kill.

The next day was spent using the horses to pack out all the meat. The two hunters had the meat placed in their own custom-made meat bags; they had come prepared. They were pleasant, helpful men with a wealth of experience and interesting stories of the past. This was to be their last moose hunt and I'm sure pleased it was a success.

# Black Streak

The fastest land animal in the world is the cheetah. The fastest animal in North America over a short distance, I believe, is the fisher. The fisher's speed is achieved by his powerful short legs. I have seen this animal leap fifteen feet from a standing position. When it runs through the deep snow the fisher actually bounds, his tracks showing as a single hole in the snow, four feet apart.

The fisher is unknown to most people and rarely seen. Even people who spend a lot of time in the bush seldom see this elusive animal unless it is in a trap. The male fisher is about the same size as a small fox but without the long legs. They are mostly black with some brown near the front shoulders. The male's fur is coarser than the smaller female's, with the female furs fetching a trapper twice the money of a male. It has been a valuable fur bearer for Canadian trappers but, like his cousin the wolverine, the fisher population is quite modest. This could be due to the adult male's habit of killing the young. The female usually tries to pick a nursery den with a small entrance hole, to keep the larger males out.

"You don't know how lucky you are," I told my Michigan hunter. His first trip to Canada and we were both staring at a fisher that was looking back at us from the edge of the bush road just ahead. The fisher's curiosity satisfied, he gave one great leap, cleared the width of the road and was off in a streak.

The marten is just as fast. The red squirrel is quick and agile as he scampers from tree to tree but is no match for the pine marten. I once saw a squirrel leap across a low wet spot with a marten two feet behind it. Both disappeared into the bush. I don't think the squirrel got too far. Yes, both these animals are fast, but both live in mortal fear of the fisher.

It seems where there are many fishers, there are few marten and vice versa. Both compete for squirrels, rabbits and other small game, but the fisher is the only animal that regularly kills the porcupine with impunity. It wasn't too many years ago that the state of Oregon was paying good money for live-trapped fisher to release in their forests. Apparently, the large porcupine population there was killing too many pine trees. I've never seen a battle between a porcupine and fisher but my friend, the late Jim Gould, once did. He related to me how he snuck up on a growling, hissing noise once in the thick pine trees.

The fisher was circling the porcupine with blazing speed and the porcupine was attempting to keep his back to the attacker with limited success. The fisher was getting a few quick bites to the head of the porcupine, but the prickly guy wasn't doing too badly with his tail either. Finally, the porcupine had enough and headed up a tree—big mistake. The fisher is the best there is in the trees and he went up the opposite side of the trunk. The porcupine's flanks were left unprotected as he climbed the small pine tree. The fisher simply reached around and opened the porcupine's tender belly with his powerful jaws. The porcupine fell down to the ground and soon it was all over.

Like all weasels, the fisher is known for its courage and toughness. My son, Bernard Jr., and I once came up to one of my Muskeg River lynx sets on cold January day. This set was a

leg-hold trap equipped with rubber jaws which hold the animal but don't damage its paw. When we arrived we discovered the trap and the drag pole it was wired to were gone. The spoor led down to the frozen river. There, we were disappointed to find the signs of a struggle. The surrounding willows were bent and bit off, but there was no animal. A search in the snow found the trap with a bit of hair still in it. "What kind of animal was it, Dad?" my son asked. I told him it was either a small wolverine or a fisher. We carried on.

A short way down river I had set a baited killing-type trap (330 conibear) to catch any wolverine that might be traveling the river. The fisher's trail led in this direction and it was here that we found our fisher.

# When Bears Come to Kill

"Stand clear and I'll finish him off," I told my brother-in-law. The bear was still moving in the thick brush after my first shot. I administered the *coup de grace* and we cautiously approached the bear that had just charged us—while we were in a canoe yet! Upon examination the "he" turned out to be a "she," a sow of about 175 pounds.

We sat down over a pail of tea and a smoke to get a grip on our nerves and talk over the possibilities of why a healthy looking bear would attack us. Brian and I had been canoeing down the Salmon River of interior British Columbia to my lower cabin to bring in supplies for the winter trapping season. The river was very low as it was early October. I usually travel alone but my new brother-in-law was a city boy from Ontario and wanted to see how I made a living so he came along. He was sitting in the bow of my seventeen-foot canoe enjoying the scenery while I paddled from the stern. I had noticed a few spawned-out salmon remains on the sandbars and had just remarked how it was late for salmon to still be around when we heard splashing sounds from around the next bend. We were in about one foot of water as the river widened out to a shallow shoal from bank to bank. About fifteen yards ahead of us appeared the bear running flat out at us, spray flying from her feet. Brian, mouth agape, turned quickly to look at me. I had the only rifle and had time to pick it up, bolt in a shell and fire almost in one motion. The bear took the slug in the chest ten feet from the canoe—and Brian. The shot turned the bear instantly and it ran up the bank out of sight. "Does this happen every time you go out in the bush?" were Brian's first words.

As I stated, the bear was a healthy sow. I checked around for cubs; there were none. I checked her teats. She was dry but showed evidence of past pregnancies. Our only clue to her strange behavior was some salmon remains around the bank where she had come from. The way I figure it, she had been feeding on the fish and heard the splashing sound of our paddles. She may have thought we were another bear coming to steal her meal. Bears don't have very good eyesight and in her blind rage did not make us out for two men in a boat. In any event things happened too fast for a sensible discussion with her. Could she actually have been attacking us as men? I say yes, as it happens more frequently than most of us realize.

A few years ago my family and our friends from the Vancouver area had a harrowing experience with a bear. Our two families were on a fishing trip to a small lake fifty miles north of Prince George. The wives and children were around the campfire while we men were out fishing in the canoes. My wife shouted for me to come in as there was a bear in camp. I paddled to shore in time to see the women hustling the kids into the cabin. The bear stood his ground as I tried to shoo him away. I picked up a

lawn chair and threw it at him. The bear started to walk slowly toward me and I showed him who was boss by running into the cabin with the women. I had a single-shot Cooey .22 inside but discovered that I had only one long rifle cartridge in my pocket. Not too prepared for an old Boy Scout. I peeked out the cabin door at the bear forty feet away and cautiously stepped out. I stood behind a large spruce tree just outside the door. Usually a black bear can be frightened off so I shouted at him again, to no avail. I then made the mistake of throwing a rock at him. Without warning, he charged. Now, contrary to the movie image showing bears charging while growling and roaring on their hind legs, this animal was all business. Ears back, head low, the black bear came at me like a streak without a sound. At three feet I shot into his forehead with one hand on the rifle and the rest of my body behind the tree. At the shot the bear turned into a contorted twist and began roaring and pawing his head furiously. He then crawled over a log and began to bite the ground and gnash his teeth. There was a double-bitted ax leaning against the cabin wall. I grabbed it and, keeping the log between me and the bear, swung the ax with two hands as hard as I could into his head. By now, my fishing partner had arrived on the scene and ran to his duffle bag in the truck where he had a semiautomatic .22. He loaded it and pumped five shots into the bear, as it was still showing faint signs of life.

It's amazing how a bear attack concentrates one's mind; only with everything over could I hear the sound of crying coming from the cabin and my heart thumping in my ears. We rolled the bear over; it was a boar of about 175 pounds. What provoked the attack? We found a few squawfish remains on the shore. Perhaps, as on the Salmon River, he was guarding his meal; he definitely knew we were humans (not a bear's normal prey). He probably had never seen a man. I've learned never to trust a bear.

Over my many years of guiding clients for both grizzly and black bears, I've had to follow up many wounded bears. Even a normally timid black bear can have a sudden shift in personality when he's got a bad belly ache and someone keeps pushing him along when he wants to rest and lick his wounds. Wounded bears seem to find the thickest willows in which to hide in these circumstances and a "would-be" guide had better be on full alert if he wants to collect old age pension.

I was on the trail of one such bear in the spring of 1983 and dusk was making its appearance with every shadow being a bear. In this instance, I was doing a heck of a lot of looking and not much walking. I was scanning with my eyes all around and directing most of my attention about thirty feet ahead. I don't know why but out of the bottom of my eye I saw a dark shape that caused me a double take. I stared at the ground about ten feet in front of me and suddenly made out a bear's head and eyes looking back at me! My rifle was at my side and that slow motion trip up to my shoulder was the longest of my life. The bear's beady eyes never moved from mine. He was laying crouched with back feet under his belly and front legs straight out front. I was sure the bear could hear my heart beat and see the blood-hot glow from my ears. I shot the instant his forehead was in the sight. He never moved at the shot but slowly straightened out his hind legs as I bolted a fresh round into my .270. A second shot was not necessary.

After I skinned the animal, I discovered the original shot had taken out one side of his diaphragm and the top of his liver. This was just a little too far back on the animal for a good kill. Would he have had the energy for a deadly spring at me? I guess I'll never know.

In the spring of the year, between May 20 and June 10, the moose in my area have their calves. At this time some bears decide they've had enough grass and clover and go looking for fresh meat. I think these moose killers get their start by eating the afterbirth when they are still young bears. They soon realize how easy it is to catch newborn calves. Many moose have twins each year, but by fall hunters will see only a single calf with the cow. The B.C. game biologists are concerned with the predation of moose calves by the large number of bears in central B.C.

My neighbor witnessed firsthand the *modus operandi* of a bear attacking a moose in the spring of 1991. He and his wife were looking out their kitchen window one morning enjoying the sight of a cow moose with a wobbly-legged newborn calf at her side. As the moose stepped out into the sheep pasture from the thick brush, the calf drew about twenty paces away from the cow. The couple then spotted a dark object in the bush and suddenly a bear rushed out full speed up to the calf. It flattened the little guy with one blow from his paw, instantly grabbed him with his mouth and ran into the bush before the dumbfounded cow moose could move.

Many people are surprised to learn that bears are cannibalistic. In the spring of 1994, I was guiding two hunters for bear when we came across the gutted carcass of a small bear of about two years of age. The signs indicated it had been killed by a much larger bear, likely a boar, but the carcass was only partially eaten. It is a known fact that when a sow bear breeds every two years she generally drives her old cubs off or sneaks away while they are preoccupied. Sometimes she is not successful and when mating season comes in June, any cub found by a boar will be killed. Some old-timers I have guided with claim a grizzly boar will kill the first-year cubs so the sow will come into heat for him. I believe this activity makes young bears very jumpy.

I was once watching the mountain slopes near the headwaters of the Stikine River with two goat hunters when we witnessed a comical sight. Periodically, we would glass the remains of a large moose we had taken two days earlier on the lower part of the mountain. A medium-sized grizzly appeared and very cautiously approached the kill. The bear did a great deal of looking around and smelled the air for about twenty minutes before it began to feed. Every few bites he would stop and look carefully around. Suddenly he bolted and ran flat out across the slope to the edge of the timber and stopped. We glassed all around and only saw a few small rocks falling from the hill above. The very nervous bear took a long time to feed again. He no doubt had a narrow escape before with a bigger bear and was on edge.

The most dangerous place to be is between a mother and her cub. I like to shoot squirrels on sunny days in early November as they are easy to see and hear, even though their pelts are not quite prime yet. I was using my single-shot .22 with shorts. Hearing a scratching sound, I looked up and saw two cubs climbing a tree. Oh, oh! Where's the mom? Over to my right about twenty yards away was the sow black bear. As I started to slowly back up, she began to emit a low moaning sound, alternately shifting her weight between each front leg and swaying her head back and forth. Bears sometimes psyche themselves up for a charge and I knew I had better vamoose fast! I managed to back out of this one all right but figure I lost another one of my nine lives over it.

# Wolverine Tales

There are not many trappers in northern B.C. who haven't had a problem with wolverine at one time or another. This animal has caused me considerable trouble over the years as well.

At times it can seem very easy to catch a wolverine and a new trapper may wonder what all the fuss is about. If there is one animal that learns fast it's old "skunk bear." It seems he only has to get nipped by cold steel once and he never forgets. I had a trap-smart wolverine dog my trails for a month in the winter of 1989. This beggar would help himself to my marten baits and knock about half the boxes off the trees in the process. He would approach a cubby set for a lynx and paw snow onto the number three jump traps I had out front. When he had snapped the traps, he helped himself to the beaver carcass inside.

I thought I'd be smart. I put a 330 conibear, a large killing-type trap, at the entrance to a cubby and set the leghold traps about eighteen inches in front. I then camouflaged them with balsam boughs. He tripped the legholds, ignored the 330 and opened a hole near the back of the cubby and helped himself. All right. I set a 330 over this new hole too. Wrong! He opened a new hole opposite from the first and demolished the whole set without getting caught. By then it was getting late in January so I conceded defeat and pulled my traps.

Not long after this experience I was talking to an Indian in Fort St. James. He told me how, in the old days, the only way to catch a smart wolverine was to rig up set gun at the back of the cubby on a trip wire to the bait. The Royal Canadian Mounted Police might have something to say about this idea today. I've heard of trappers who were faced with either losing the entire trapping season or eliminating the problem. They would weld up a large baited treble hook and hang it up off the ground about four feet. The wolverine would jump up in the air to grab the bait and would gaff himself. Fortunately, today this sort of practice is against the law and no ethical trapper would resort to this tactic.

A lot has been said of the courage of wolverines. I once caught a wolverine in a leghold that had been set for a lynx. It was one of the new offset traps and was wired to a four-inch-thick pole six feet long. When the wolverine saw me coming at him he tried to run off through the willows, but the drag slowed him down. I took a shot at his head with my .22 and missed. At the shot, flight turned into fight, and the animal turned and came for me. I didn't miss with my second shot.

The fellow who trapped the Muskeg fifty years before me had a bad time once with a wolverine. Martin Shaffer seldom carried a rifle; when he caught anything large, he would cut himself a club to dispatch the animal. This would work with a lynx, but once, a wolverine he caught kept dodging around so Martin decided to pin the animal and choke him with his knee and hands. It didn't work out as planned and a trip to the hospital was required, as well as new clothes; the old ones were shredded.

I guided for several years in the mountains around Tatlatui Park, and it is here on the slopes above timberline that a person can watch wolverines at work. This is an animal that never seems to slow down to walk; he always seems to lope along even if the hill is steep. I recall a time two hunters and I were watching about twenty caribou grazing and moving along an alpine slope when a movement caught my eye. On a dry creek bed, what at first looked like two wolves, turned out to be two wolverines. The creek bed went almost straight up the mountain and the wolverines were following it up at a fast pace. They never stopped once and ran over the crest of the mountain out of sight. They were in our sight for about five minutes and traveled 2,000 feet up and over the ridge. It would have taken about thirty minutes for a man in good shape to make the same climb.

One spring day, another guide and I were watching for grizzly on the open slopes of the mountain across from camp. Three mountain goats, a billy, a nanny and a small kid, were feeding on the new grass above tree line. As there were no bears to be seen, I decided to fix up a pot of tea. Just about the time the water was boiling, my partner shouted, "Bernie, come and look at the two wolverines!" They looked to be two full-sized adults and they made a beeline for the billy goat. The goat, who had his head down, didn't see them until they were about fifty feet from him.

You don't see goats run too often but this one did. He was trying to get to a small cliff on the shoulder of the mountain and had about 100 yards to travel. The lead wolverine caught up to the goat and climbed part way up its back; the other wolverine was trying to bite the goat's back quarters. The goat carried the

 one piggyback for a bit then stumbled and all three animals rolled. The goat got up fast and with a spurt of speed made the cliff with the wolverines on his tail. The goat then walked out on a narrow ledge that looked more like a crack in the rock face. He turned to look back at the two wolverines who now knew they were beat. They ran off to look for easier prey.

I trapped with the late Jim Gould during the winter of 1978. He had many experiences with wolverines during his years on the trapline. He once showed me a long-spring trap that had both steel springs broken. A large male wolverine had broken them with his jaws to escape!

How large do wolverines get? I weighed a big male I'd caught at twenty-nine pounds. I've heard of thirty-five pounders and I read once that in prehistoric times there was a wolverinelike animal that weighed 300 pounds. That animal would have given those cavemen trappers something to think about!

# Of Horses and Hunting

A dog may be man's best friend around home but a horse takes over this title in the wild mountains of B.C. The horse is a reasonably surefooted animal that will carry a man all day to places he could not logistically reach by himself. The backbreaking job of packing into the best remote spots is a piece of cake when old Dobbin does the hard work.

In the early 1980s, I made several trips, using horses, to the Johansen Lake area to hunt mountain game. This is, in my opinion, the most spectacular area in B.C. The towering peaks easily rival those in Banff and Jasper. On our most memorable trip, my younger brother Dan accompanied me and a neighbor friend, Mel Ohlen. Now, trucking the horses (we had six on this trip) the 250 miles from Prince George was an adventure in itself. Once we left the Hart Highway near Windy Point we still had 170 miles of rough gravel road to cover.

The steepest grades are found to the north of Aiken Lake, and it was there that we ran into trouble. The road climbed up a very steep grade. I was pulling the four-horse trailer with my pickup truck when a trailer tire blew out. I stopped, but every time the horses moved the entire rig began to slip backwards on the loose shale. The roadbed was sloping at an angle toward the 200-foot drop off and we were getting dangerously close to the edge. After some anxious moments the two men got the tires blocked while I stayed on the brakes. We changed the tire and, with all four tires on my 4 x 4 scratching, we were again on our way.

We unloaded our horses along Johansen Lake and were soon on our way to Asika Lake, about a ten-mile ride. We arrived at an old outfitter's camp. I had heard that the guiding area had just changed owners and was not in use this year so we took over the cabin. The next three days were spent riding, hunting and just exploring the Asika River area.

One morning my brother Dan had a mishap with his horse. I was leading when we came upon a blowdown laying over the trail. My horse just stepped over it because the log wasn't too high. Dan was riding "Old Bill," an appaloosa that, instead of stepping over, jumped it. Dan was unprepared for the sudden lunge and fell off onto the ground. He landed on his rump right on a rock. I tied up the horses and went back to see Dan groaning on the ground. Apparently he had landed on his sciatic nerve and he had no feeling in his right leg. We were several miles from camp. After about an hour the feeling started to return and, with difficulty, Dan climbed back on for the painful ride back. He spent the next two days recuperating around camp.

While Dan was laid up, I decided to explore the Sustut Lake country. The Sustut is a picturesque, long lake with towering mountains surrounding it, and I saw several mountain goats feeding on the cliffs. As I walked my horse along the beach I could see the remains of spawned out salmon. A little later, I spotted a silver-tipped grizzly feeding above timberline. After a two-hour climb by foot I managed to get close enough to take a shot. The bear never knew what hit him when I fired my .270. The next day, all three of us climbed up. Dan wasn't really in shape to do much packing, but he wanted to see that grizzly! Mel and I carried the hide, with the head still attached, back to where we had the horses tied in the timber and then the rodeo began.

Now, a horse has a natural fear of bears even if they have never seen one. All four of the horses we had with us rolled their eyes back and pulled on their lead ropes as we approached with that smelly hide. I finally had to blindfold my palomino and rub some bear blood on his nostrils. After a few minutes I slipped the tied-up hide onto the saddle. The rest of the trip back to camp went smoothly.

The next day was our last in camp and was spent skinning the bear hide clean and salting it down. One horse had thrown a shoe so we fixed that also. Late that afternoon we heard horse bells. Twelve horses, three guides and two American hunters came into camp. After a few awkward words we told them we would pull out while they unpacked. We would pitch our tents a mile up the valley at a good camping spot and let the rightful owners take over the cabin.

They told us it took them three hours to pack their horses up and about two hours to ride in. We had been on the trail for a week and were feeling pretty good about our horse packing ability. I whispered to Dan and Mel, "Let's show these fellas how expert we are. I'll bet we could pack up and be on our way in fifteen minutes." We were slick and fast as we put the pack saddles on and threw a diamond hitch over each of the three pack animals. I even carefully set our big pot of beans that we had warmed on the stove for supper right on the top pack under the canvas. I could see the other party looking at us out of the corner of their eye once in a while. Yes, we were a smug group of cowboys as we climbed up into the saddle in less than fifteen minutes. I started out in the lead and waved goodbye to the newcomers. Dan was spurring his horse but it wouldn't budge. It was then that one stranger hollered over to us, "You'd better take the hobbles off that horse, he'll probably go better." Dan looked down at his horse's feet and sure enough he had forgotten to remove the hobbles. With red faces, we slunk out of camp. Oh, I almost forgot to mention we had only made it a quarter mile when that pot of beans shifted and the packhorse bucked it off over his head.

# Taming the Beast

His loping stride, almost bounding, was easy to see in the deep snow. The wolverine trail was not a welcome sight. The previous week he had raided my chunk of bacon that I had in a wooden box on the porch of my cabin. I was lucky he hadn't gained entry into the cabin. I have heard stories of the damage they can do when inside a trapper's shack and of the smell that they leave behind. One of this devil's tricks is to tear off the stove pipe and roof jack to get inside. My next four trap locations had been robbed of bait and the traps had been sprung. This was a wise old wolverine. I set a few snares for him but to no avail. I then set out the wolverine's favorite dish—skunk. I had caught this smelly cousin of the wolverine in a leg trap a few days before and had not got around to skinning it yet. The skunk's only real enemy besides rabies and man is the wolverine. The wolverine hunts them down with ease as the skunk is a relatively slow customer. The skunk's smell is not disagreeable to the wolverine as he is just a big skunk himself. Alas, even the skunk bait was turned down by this troublemaker. I was not sorry to see him eventually leave my area—probably to bother another trapper further west.

A friend and fellow trapper had been into a lake on his trapline two weeks before and had noticed more than sixty muskrat push-ups on the ice. These push-ups are where the muskrats haul green vegetation up from the bottom of the lake and pile it up around a hole in the ice that they make. These piles are domed over with mud and the muskrat can climb up inside to eat his meal and still be out of the weather and safe from predators like the mink.

Now, the trapper returned with his traps hoping to cash in on all those muskrats. He drove his snowmobile to the first push-up and noticed it had been opened and the hole had frozen over. The tracks around were indistinct, but he figured a moose had pawed the top off for the greens inside. Moose do this often, especially in late winter when they are tired of a steady twig diet. But wait! The next push-up was torn up also and the next. In fact, almost all had been disturbed. Blood stains, bits of muskrat hide and a few bones lay about the ice. Slowly the trapper put together, from the evidence written in the snow, what had happened—wolverine. This overgrown weasel was using his brains for this caper. Tearing off the frozen mud from the top of the push-up, the wolverine lay quietly with his belly over the hole. The muskrat, who dove under the ice when the wolverine started, would come back and see his hole still looking dark, as it should. When the little guy climbed up to his ledge, the wolverine would feel the muskrat touch his belly hairs and then he would spin down to catch him—end of muskrat.

The wolverine does have a bad rap sheet and I've been as guilty as any when it comes to maligning this carnivore. I recently had my eyes opened to the wolverine's playful side, however. My brother Pat and I annually travel to Portland, Oregon, where we set up a display booth to book hunters. The show takes place in a large Exposition Center, and in 1994 the show featured an exhibition of two wolverines and a large timber wolf. All three animals were raised in captivity and the wolverines were huge, forty-five pounds each. The trainer could handle all these animals and would pick up the wolverines and play with them; they seemed to enjoy the attention. At show time, the wolf was let into the large enclosed area with the wolverines. A chunk of

41

ice the size of a forty-five-gallon drum had been placed in the cage and on this the two wolverines lay to cool off. When the wolf (a large specimen himself) was let into the wolverines' compound, the two big weasels were instantly alert with one animal crouched down, claws braced into the ice block. The wolf, hackles up, cautiously circled the two wolverines perched on the block. The wolf's circle became smaller and smaller until he passed very near the block. The one wolverine had a wicked look in his eye and after the wolf's third pass he leaped onto the wolf's back and dug his claws into his sides. The wolf rolled over with a growl, and, to my surprise, the two of them began to play like two dogs.

The trainer then threw in a large piece of meat and the wolf grabbed it instantly. One wolverine, not to be outdone, grabbed the other end of the meat and the two animals started a tug-of-war, all the while growling and snarling to the delight of the audience. It was amazing to see how playful these normally wild animals, mortal enemies in nature, had become.

# Fourth Time Lucky

Dennis seemed like a nice guy. I had just introduced myself as his guide for the next ten days and we were getting to know one another over coffee in the cook shack.

Our hunting area was the big mountain country in and around Tatlatui Park in northern B.C. I was working for Love Bros. & Lee Outfitters at the time (1986). Dennis said, "I sure hope you can get me a moose." I replied that I would try my best and figured we should be successful as the rut was in full swing. "Is this your first time moose hunting in Canada?" I asked. Dennis said, "As a matter of fact no, I have been three times before." I asked him if he had any luck on these previous hunts and he had not. "Just not seeing them?" I asked. It turned out he had seen many shootable bulls on his past hunts. "To tell you the truth, Bernard, I get the shakes so bad I can't hit anything when I'm hunting and yet I'm an excellent shot at the range on paper targets." Well, he was being perfectly honest with me and at least I knew what I was up against—a man who knew his limitations.

It was the day two of the hunt before we saw our first moose or, I should say, I saw it as Dennis was having a hard time picking it out in the willows where it stood facing us. In fairness, I was lucky enough to see it enter from the lake edge and Dennis had not. We poled the riverboat quietly toward shore and, at 100 yards, I was trying to point the moose out to Dennis when Bullwinkle bolted for parts unknown. There was no time for a shot. We returned to camp that afternoon a little disappointed.

The next two days were rainy and windy, and we saw no moose. This is not uncommon as moose get jumpy when large lake waves are crashing into shore and they lose half of their main line of defense, namely their hearing.

Day five dawned clear and frosty and we figured the moose should be active after two days of holing up. We decided to leave

43

the lake and try our luck on a series of swampy meadows about a half-mile walk from camp. I had seen moose there on the previous hunt.

About fifteen minutes out from camp we cautiously approached the lip of a cutbank that overlooked Bird Creek. There was a middlin' size bull feeding on the willows not thirty yards below us. He must have heard our approach because he was looking directly at us. "Boy! That's good enough for me!" Dennis said and attempted to chamber a round into his 30-06. His rifle was a Remington semiautomatic and one pull back on the side lever gets the rifleman ready to fire. Somehow Dennis, in his excitement, didn't pull the lever all the way back and a round got caught halfway between the magazine and the chamber. While Dennis was furiously working the action on his rifle the bull decided he'd had enough of us and loped off to the safety of the tall timber. Oh well.

The morning was young and the best openings were still ahead of us. The second meadow was empty of wildlife except for a couple of whiskey jacks flitting ahead of us as we walked. Another half hour of walking and we were approaching the timber edge that looked out on a twenty-acre meadow. I whispered to Dennis to be as quiet as possible. There were lots of fresh moose beds the last time I was here and we might get lucky.

The area looked empty but we stayed put and carefully glassed the forest edge all around. After about ten minutes Dennis spotted movement and three moose stepped out into the open. Two cows led a good bull out of the trees and stopped about 200 yards from us. We had to advance about another twenty yards to reach a bald knoll and a clear view of the moose. After the previous fiasco, Dennis had asked if I minded him chambering a round and carrying the rifle on safe. I minded, but not enough to say no. He was a safe hunter. Dennis was ready with a round chambered and the safety on.

This location had one drawback. There was no place to rest the rifle for a steady shot, so Dennis decided to try offhand. After a minute of waving his barrel around he decided to shoot from a prone position as there was no grass in the way and this would steady the rifle. He lay down to try this idea but discovered that his stiff neck (an old injury) prevented him from lifting his head high enough to see down the barrel. We were still messing around with shooting positions when the wind abruptly changed directions. Oh, oh. The three moose had their heads up sniffing, and in about the time it takes to say "rats" all three were off and jogging for the bush. Round two went to the moose. Dennis looked at me with disappointment on his face.

By now it was 11:00 A.M., the sun had long since melted off the frost and it was beginning to get warm. We had just about used up the best hunting time for the morning. I said, "Dennis, there's still one more meadow about fifteen minutes ahead and we might as well check it out before we turn back."

Again we pussyfooted up to the edge of this last meadow. Now you talk about luck! There standing smack dab in the middle of a twenty-acre opening was the biggest bull so far! "Man, that's just what I'm after!" whispered Dennis, excitedly. "I don't want to screw up this time. Do you think I can get closer?" We had a perfect wind in our face, the moose hadn't heard us, and hadn't a clue we were near. We cut the range to 150 yards and stopped at a small log to rest. I laid my pack down and Dennis settled in for a shot. Or should I say shots. That semiautomatic fired four rounds before the echo from the first round ended. I had the binoculars on the moose during the shooting and saw no hits. The bull raised his head and I'm sure was wondering if it was going to rain with all this thunder. Dennis had a second clip that was already loaded up in his pocket, ready to go, so he slammed it in and got ready to shoot again. Bam. Bam. Bam. Bam. The moose was starting to look nervous but I saw no hit. "Take it easy, Dennis, and take your time with each shot," I said. A third clip appeared from his down vest pocket. I had the feeling Dennis was used to laying down a lot of lead. Four more shots punched holes in the scenery. Dennis started to load up a new clip and the moose started to high step it to the tall timber but stopped just at the edge. "Now squeeze slowly and concentrate," I said to Dennis. Bang. Nothing. Bang. Nothing. Bang, and I saw the moose's front leg buckle. Instantly on three legs the moose leaped for the bush just as Dennis got off his last shot. "Did I get him?" he asked. "He's leg shot," I said.

Now Dennis was shaking bad and feeling bad. "Wounding an animal is the last thing I wanted," he said. "I feel real bad." I pulled out a cigar and lit up. "It'll take twenty minutes for me to finish this smoke, Dennis, and then we'll go have a look." I knew from experience that a moose will not go far when he's wounded. But, once the hunter spooks him from his bed, if he's not finished off, he will go for miles before laying down again. A moose is in trouble with a hind leg out, but with only one front leg, a moose can run like a three-legged dog all day.

We crossed the meadow to where we last saw the moose and I picked up a blood trail. I was in the lead and had only gone seventy-five yards into the bush when I saw a big set of antlers above the willows. Here was our moose. He had a nice spread of antlers with lots of points. Dennis was one happy guy. When we quartered the animal, we discovered that Dennis's last shot (number sixteen) had nicked the lower part of the lungs—a fatal shot after all.

Dennis returned home to Minnesota three days later loaded down with meat and horns. I had skinned out the head so he could get a full shoulder head mount done. He can now look up on the wall and remember his "fourth time lucky" hunt.

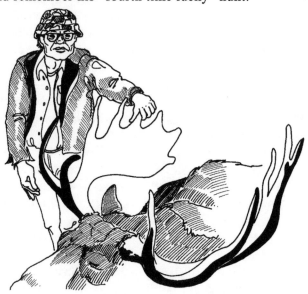

# Freezing Death

Oh, I was pretty careful around thin ice. I always undid the bindings on my snowshoes when walking up rivers so that if I broke through I could kick them off easily. I always carried a long spike in my parka pocket to help pull myself up onto the ice. I often cut a long pole to carry when crossing lakes, with their usual blow holes and weak spots that could drown a man.

Trapping season starts for land fur on the first of November. The problem is the lakes usually don't freeze solidly until November 15 or 20. The pine marten run is at its peak during this month. A good trapper takes 90 percent of his marten catch before the hard cold and deep snows of December force the marten to hunt under the snow for mice.

I was pushing my luck. There were four to five inches of ice on Jim Lake, where I had about eight marten traps to set around the shore. I checked the thickness with my ax and decided if I kept my snowmobile close to shore there should be no problem—there wasn't, at first.

The lake was about a mile long with a "dog leg" in it. I was sledding around a point of land half way down the lake and doing about thirty mph when I felt my machine breaking through. I was about twenty yards from shore. As the machine broke through, I leapt off in an attempt to reach the unbroken ice. I didn't make it. I hit the solid ice around the hole with my face. The water was about five and a half feet deep. I am six feet tall and could just keep my face above water when standing on my toes. I managed on my first try to jump up a little and crawl up on the two-inch-thick ice. As long as I lay on it, the ice held, and I slithered to shore like a snake. I was soaked thoroughly and my teeth were chattering behind lips that looked like an African Ubangi's. On the plus side, I still had my pack on my back with an ax in it and my waterproof matches were in my pocket along with a candle.

47

Thank God for spruce trees with their long dry lower branches. I lit the candle with shaking hands and soon had a roaring fire going. Two things were in my favor. The temperature was only a few degrees below freezing and I was wearing wool clothes. I stripped down to my long johns and wrung out my wool pants and shirt. The next three hours were spent drying out around the fire.

Things didn't look good for my snowmobile down in that black cold hole. I dressed and chopped down a large dry pine snag, skidded it to shore and pushed it out on the ice. Still short of the hole, I cut another and pushed it out, too.

Soon I was standing on my bridge looking down the hole. Using a stick with a hooked crotch, I managed to hook a ski. I slowly pulled the machine to shore breaking the ice in front of it as I went and keeping myself on top of the log bridge. When the snowmobile began to come out of the water it was heavy and I had to get wet again. I stood in the thigh deep water and wrestled the water logged machine to shore, then spent another hour in front of the fire.

After I'd dried myself out, I did the same for the spark plug. I pulled the starter cord until all the water squirted from the cylinder and then I replaced the plug. About 100 pulls later the old machine fired up and I ran it to drier land. I then left the machine where it sat and snowshoed out. A week later the lake had frozen solid and I could drive my machine home. After this close call I had a much-increased respect for thin ice.

Others have not been as lucky as I. I guided for Art Bracey Outfitters in the 1970s and he related to me the story of his father-in-law, Harry Clayton.

Harry was a good trapper who knew what he was doing. He knew how to read ice. He had to, because his trapline was around Chief Lake. Like all bigger lakes there were always blow holes appearing after a heavy snow fall. These are places where the weight of the snow pushing down on the ice forces the lake water through cracks to the surface. The rising water erodes the ice for several feet around the hole and open water results. A cold night can put only a skim of ice over the hole. If it doesn't snow again, these spots are easy to see because of the clear ice contrasting with the white snow-covered ice surrounding it. The problem arises when a skiff of snow or hoarfrost makes these holes hard to see.

Harry had left for home one Christmas season night. His friends and family wanted him to wait until morning as his route would have to cross Chief Lake. That was the last time anybody saw Mr. Clayton alive. His body was found in the spring. His finger nails were worn off from clawing at the ice trying to get out. This was a tragedy and a warning to all trappers to always be careful on ice.

# Fighting Bulls

We saw the bull circling a small grove of trees far above us at timberline. "There's something wrong with that moose's leg," I told my two hunters. The animal was walking stiff-legged, and then I saw it, a second bull moose a short distance in the grove. The first bull was using a show-off technique I'd not seen before. We continued to watch as both big bulls squared off against one another; watching was all we could do though, as it was too late in the afternoon for a stalk.

The two hunters had a hard time sleeping that night with the thoughts of what was to come tomorrow. One man had already taken a good fifty-inch bull but would be going along to take photos and just to be in on the excitement. We were up and fed before daybreak but the moose were gone. "I don't think they'll go far as there's likely a cow near by," I told them.

It took two hours to reach the site of the previous day's battle with still no sign of the moose. We sat on a rock outcropping that commanded a good view all around. We heard the bulls before we saw them. Clack, clack. It took a few minutes to locate the source but there they were, 300 yards below us. This was not the first time I'd seen moose fighting but not like this. Moose usually stand shoulder to shoulder and rake each other in the side. I've seen moose with broken ribs from this tactic. Sometimes they will lock horns and shove each other around, but these two were also backing up four or five feet from each other and colliding with such terrific force we could hear them clearly from our perch.

We descended to within excellent shooting range, about thirty yards, and climbed on top of a house-sized boulder. Both bulls were still preoccupied. With our excellent ringside seat we watched the battle royal.

The moose had chosen a dry creek bed to settle matters. With heads lowered and antlers locked they were taking turns pushing each other back and forth, sometimes falling to their knees. Small bushes and trees were bent or snapped off around the site. The moose were breathing hard from this exertion and their breath was rising like steam in the cold morning air. One animal managed to get better footing and drove the other back and around in a circle. He then finished the charge by ramming his adversary in the ribs, forcing out a big grunt.

"Which is the biggest one?" my hunter asked. Both looked good but I liked the spikes and the large palms on the antlers of the nearest moose. With a solid rest over my backpack, he fired his .270. I could see hair fly from just behind the moose's shoulder, a good solid hit. Both bull moose just stood there and looked at us as a cow stepped into the open for the first time. "Hold your fire," I said. "You got him good." The bull still showed no sign of the hit and walked calmly over a knoll and out of sight.

The wind continued from the two remaining moose to us and neither of the animals moved a muscle. "Go on, get!" I shouted, but the bull's blood was up, along with his hackles, and there was

51

no way he would move. I knew better than to crowd him. My hunter and I began to throw rocks and shout at the big guy. Finally, after we'd bounced a few good ones off him (we were safely on top of our boulder), he ran off taking the cow with him.

We cautiously approached the knoll where we last saw the stricken moose and there he was, a beautiful specimen. His antlers were over fifty-four inches across with big palms having lots of points. I'm sure this moose weighed close to 1,700 pounds. His neck was swollen from the rut and two tines had been broken from his antlers, probably from the fight. When we skinned him out, we discovered he had one broken rib.

One of the strangest stories about fighting moose I've ever heard happened on the Parsnip River in the early 1960s, before the W. A. C. Bennett Dam flooded the country. The guide, a friend of mine, was hunting by riverboat. He and the hunter with him stopped for lunch on a small island in the river. They had just stepped onto the beach when they heard a moose grunt. Stepping into the cottonwoods to have a look, they could see a moose that looked like an elk, that is, his antlers looked like an elk's. The moose had no palmation, just two great spikes that rose off his head for over three feet. With each step the moose let out a grunt and, picking up speed, charged the two men. Both men fired at once and dropped him in his tracks.

Later that day in the settlement of Finlay Forks (now gone) they unloaded the moose onto shore. An old Sikanni Indian was among the small crowd watching the unloading. The old timer said to the guide, after seeing the moose, "Hm, him fighting bull." The hunter got the following story out of the wise old Indian. It was still a large bodied moose but, plain to see, he was well past his prime. The gray hind legs and the particularly odd antlers suggested an old animal, probably well into his teens. He was likely the cock of the walk in his younger days, but now he was being beaten in every fight with the younger bulls. This old warrior retreated to a secluded spot to nurse his wounds and at the approach of anything he would charge. This was exactly what happened when the two men landed on the island.

# The Beginner

When a young man goes hunting for the first time with his dad there is no shortage of optimism. I can remember my early expeditions with dad like they were yesterday. Now, looking back on it, I realize my dad, Dan, was not really a hunter. In fact, he used to have a hard time when it came to slaughtering the rabbits we raised. He took me hunting because, even at fifteen years of age, I was gung ho for the sport. Although we didn't collect a deer, we had a good time and often when we get together we talk about our trip to the North Thompson country.

We were driving our number one bush rig, a 1950 Plymouth car. It was getting dark as we traveled north of Kamloops and it was time to look for a camp spot to pitch our tent. We settled for a spot alongside the highway in the big ponderosa pines. There wasn't a lot of competition for camping sites back in 1962. In fact, we never saw another hunter for the next four days of our long weekend hunt.

I woke up before dad (his snoring was awesome) and went outside to see the squirrel that was scolding us. I decided to go after the squirrel for fun and started to climb the lone pine tree he was on. As I moved up, he moved up, until seventy feet off the ground I couldn't

go up any further on the skinny treetop. About this time, dad emerged from the tent and when I waved at him from on high the squirrel above me panicked and jumped for the ground. He free-fell spread-eagled and hit with a thump on his belly. He managed to run to the next tree and, once safely up, really began to swear at us in squirrel language. Dad was killing himself with laughter.

In the morning we started up a steep logging road and when it began to get too rough for our rig we carried on by foot. Dad stayed on the road while I beat the bush below for deer. The sun was warm and dad decided to catch a few winks with his back against the road bank. I must have spooked a deer for dad woke up to a thrashing sound and looked up just as a big buck jumped over his head and out of sight. That was as close as we came to deer for the entire trip.

We camped that evening up on the mountain by the car. Around midnight the rain began and an hour later it really began to pour. Dad got up to check the tent and came back in with a concerned look on his face. "I'm worried the road might wash out," he said, "we'd better pack up and drive down off this hill." I guess neither of us were paying much attention to the side roads that were entering as we drove up the previous day. We came to a fork and took the wrong one. "I don't recall this road being quite so steep," dad said. The next thing we knew, we were going down a skid trail we had no hope of ever getting back up. The trail petered out in a washed out creek bed and we were stuck. The night was black, the rain coming down in sheets, we were lost, and now we were forced to spend the night in the car, on a 30° angle.

I've spent more comfortable nights, but dawn eventually came and with it welcome sunshine. Only now could we really see the fix we were in. We started down the creek bed hoping to find the main road again. We had only gone a short way when a log cabin, perched on the bank, came into view. A knock on the door produced a voice in a foreign tongue that dad took for "come in." Inside was an old Chinese man who invited us, in English, to come in and sit down. It turns out this old timer had been there for fifty years and picked pine cones that he sold as Christmas decorations to department stores to supplement his old age pension. He showed us pictures of his relations back in Communist China whom he hoped would one day be free to come and see him. He made us breakfast and Chinese tea and then came to give us a hand with our car. We brought along his picks and shovels. He did a little prospecting and also picked pine cones.

The work took us most of the morning but we leveled out the creek bed well enough to ease the car down to the cabin and out to the main road. The old man insisted we again join him for lunch and he even worked out a cleaning rag I had earlier gotten stuck in my rifle. His hospitality and help were the most memorable parts of our trip.

Dad and I went on a few more hunts together and, no, we never did bag an animal on any of them, but I'll never forget that first trip.

# Hooves of Iron

Never mind the bull, it's the cow moose that is the most dangerous. When a man gets between a cow and her calf, he's asking for trouble. I know a fellow that spent the better part of the morning sitting up a tree while a cow moose tore up the ground below him, and he had been lucky to even make the tree.

For about fifteen years we have had a "calf moose only" season in the area north of Prince George. It goes without saying that there is usually a cow nearby. I was hunting for meat to feed my family one October day in 1983 and was quietly watching the shore line of a small lake when two moose, a cow and calf, appeared on the far shore. The distance was quite far, so I used an old rotten log for a rest and got off a shot at the calf. Both animals spun around and walked into the timber out of sight. I wasn't sure if I had connected or not but walked the three-quarters of a mile around the lake head to check for blood. A hunter should always do this as sometimes a moose shows no outward sign of being shot.

When I got to the spot where the moose had stood I began tracking, still no blood. I had covered the bush area that extended a short way back from the lake shore when I heard a moose bark. This is an alarm call that cow moose make at a pursuer or to bring their calf up to them and out of danger. I then saw the calf laying dead beneath a tree. The cow now appeared and began to come at me, still walking, but with her hump hairs standing straight up. I had no place to hide so I shot in the air over her head, which turned her, but she kept circling me in the jack pines as I worked on the calf. I had to fire two more times in front of her feet and it was only after I'd opened the calf, with its strange smell, that she finally left for good.

Moose are handy at using their front hooves for weapons, as many a wolf could likely attest. A neighbor of mine, Ed Austin, owned a large malamute dog, named Jigs, that weighed over 100 pounds. As Ed drove to town one winter's day, the dog rode in the pickup box. The snow was deep and the grader had plowed up high banks on either side of the road. In front, there was a moose standing on the road. Ed drove slowly with the moose reluctantly walking ahead. When they came to a pull-out the moose left the road and walked a few yards out into the deep snow. It was then the dog got brave and, leaping out of the truck, ran at the moose. The moose turned and before Jigs could get away the cow pummeled him with her front legs. The dog desperately tried to get away but was badly bruised and cut up before he made the truck. Jigs was lucky to be alive and lazed around the house for two weeks recuperating from the ordeal.

A canoe in shallow water is a poor spot to be when a moose charges. It was just such a predicament my brother-in-law, Mickey Armstrong, and I found ourselves in, one autumn day. We were moose hunting on the Muskeg River which is more of a stream than a river during the fall. Just a short way down from our launch site we encountered a cow and calf moose standing on shore. It was calf season so we both shot. The calf fell off the bank into the river; the cow took off. As we were tying the dead moose to the canoe, the cow reappeared downstream and looked to be in an ugly mood. "Watch her, Mick," I said and then she charged us. I had along a shotgun for ducks and brought this into play. I fired in front of the moose, water spraying her in the face, to no effect. In desperation I shot her in the chest with the bird shot. This turned her and she ran the few feet to the bank. She was deciding whether to try us again when I gave her another broadside. She finally left. I doubt the shot did her any permanent harm as she was about thirty yards away when I shot her and I was using light loads; a moose has a tough hide.

When the snow lays deep, don't crowd a moose. I learned this the hard way one February. I had my entire family in our old Ford car one morning as we drove to Prince George. We had just pulled out of our driveway when a moose appeared up ahead on the road. The snow banks were high, the roadway narrow, and there was not much room to get around the moose. Hugging one side of the road as close as I dared, I drove slowly past the standing moose. Just when we were abreast, she laid her ears back and lunged at the car, striking the passenger side door with her front hooves.

Moose are formidable opponents when they feel threatened. Their size and strength combined with surprising agility serves them well as protection.

# Niven Creek

The lake gets shallow where Niven Creek flows in from the south. This stream carries a lot of silt during spring run off and the delta which forms is frequented by both moose and caribou. When I was guiding in this country I could always count on seeing game at the Niven even if all we got were some photos of a homely-headed cow moose with a mug full of lake weeds.

An Oregon hunter and I had been enjoying the antics of a courting bull moose as it tried to woo a cow one fine morning at Niven Creek. The bull was only of middlin' size so we weren't interested in shooting. The bull would approach the female with his neck stretched out and just when he tried to mount her the cow's calf would rush up and strike at this bully hurting his mama. The bull didn't take kindly to this interruption of his "manly" duty and would run the calf off, up the beach. The cow's mothering instincts would kick in and she would then turn, with ears laid back, and run at the young bull to save her calf. This romance was getting nowhere, but we were having fun watching and taking more pictures.

Another time, my boss, Bob Henderson, was flying supplies into the hunting camp and as he flew over the lake narrows at the Niven's mouth, he noticed a great stag caribou standing in the three-foot deep water 100 yards offshore. He didn't think much of the occasion until he again passed overhead four hours later and the caribou was still there. Moose will spend hours in the water, for the feed, but caribou are usually just passing through. Bob dropped down for a closer look. On both banks of the lake he saw wolves patiently waiting for the caribou to emerge from the water. Bob buzzed a group of them on one shore and drove them off. The caribou sensed the coast was clear and immediately ran for shore and freedom.

Niven Creek had been good, too, to Phil, a fireman and

paramedic in the state of California. He was retired from that job at thirty-five years of age. He had severely injured his back while attempting to carry a victim from a burning building and was now training himself to be an accountant. His severance pay was financing his first big game hunting adventure in B.C. He had earlier stated that his back, although not 100 percent, was good enough to climb the mountains for caribou or goats.

Our first day out and all was not going smoothly. The rugged mountain we were climbing was taking its toll on Phil's back. He gamely kept up but I turned on several occasions to see him wincing in pain. "Just great," Phil said, "Thirty-five hundred dollars for a mountain hunt and I can't climb any more." We were about 700 feet from the top of an alpine plateau so I told Phil to sit and rest and I would climb up to look around. He could watch me through the binoculars and if I saw anything worthwhile I would wave him up. Though the scenery was breathtaking, nothing but a porcupine could I find. We returned to camp.

In the morning, Phil's back had stiffened up badly so I used the slight drizzle of rain we were having as an excuse to spend the day around camp. The following day was sunny and calm, ideal for hunting if Phil was up to it. He solemnly told me after breakfast he would not be able to climb anymore. "We'll take the boat up to the Niven," I said, optimistically. "It's a bit early for caribou to be down this low but you never know." I doubted we would see anything but sometimes the caribou change ranges and to do so they usually cross the lake at Niven Creek.

By nine o'clock we were approaching the delta and about a quarter mile away I could see something near shore, a caribou, a bull, and not a bad set of antlers either. The bull looked as nervous as Phil and began to run out onto a sandspit. The animal then turned heel and ran for the trees along the shore. Our hopes faded as the bull disappeared into the bush. I killed the outboard and we looked and waited quietly. After about two minutes Phil turned to me and said "looks like he's gone."

Many a hunter has capitalized on the caribou's greatest weakness, his curiosity. I don't know if this caribou wanted to have another look at us, heard us talking or just decided he wanted another drink, but out of the woods he came and ran up the beach to within eighty yards. He stopped and stood staring at us. What luck! Phil didn't need any prompting from me to shoot. He fired his 7mm Magnum and the caribou took off at a dead run and a dead run it was; he only made it thirty yards before collapsing on the sand. He had an atypical set of antlers with palmation at the top and many points. Phil was more than pleased and so was I, especially considering Phil's condition. This caribou was a lucky gift and I was as excited as Phil about his good fortune.

# On the Omineca River 1981

In the spring of 1981 I built an old-fashioned riverboat out of wood. Thus began fourteen years of riverboating. Each summer I would take my family up a different river in northern B.C. just for the fun of exploring areas of the province that few have ever seen. I've chosen five of our most adventuresome trips to relate to the reader.

It was not a very auspicious beginning to my budding career as a riverboat man. Ken Christopher, an old Finlay river rat, and I had put a hole in the side of my thirty-six-foot long plywood boat and cracked a rib. We had just put the *Spirit of the Finlay* into the Nechako River under the old bridge in Prince George. Before I could get the Evinrude fired up, we drifted sideways into a barge strut the fisheries department had put up for measuring the river depths. The hole was high so we stuffed a rag in her and headed up the river for the shakedown cruise. The rest of the trip up through the White Mud rapids went smoothly and I got a feel for the boat.

Our August trip was on the historic Omineca River. This river had seen a lot of activity during the gold rush of the 1870s and again, to a lesser degree, during the depression years. We hoped to be able to get up the river to at least Old Hogum; it would depend on the water level.

August 1 saw us on the Hart Highway trailering the long boat up to Germansen Landing, our launching point. Besides my wife, Jo-Eane, and I, we had our three children, my mom and dad and our Labrador retriever, Sal. The road trip took us up the west side of Williston Lake then inland to the town of Manson Creek and finally to Germansen Landing where we put in at Westfall's Trading Post.

The Omineca looked beautiful with its emerald green water. We had just left the landing when a float plane buzzed over us heading up the river. The "hot dog" pilot steered the Beaver float plane under the bridge that crossed just ahead of us.

The weather was good and before we made camp that first night we had landed grayling, rainbows and dolly varden. The grayling on the Omenica are nice, hard-bodied fish and have a blue color to them. We caught several that weighed over a pound and a few that weighed close to two pounds; not bad when you consider that the world's record is only four pounds.

My mother, Pauline, (in her sixties) was a bit nervous about the rapids, the boat and, in particular, bears. It was on her insistence that we took the dog along as a warning at night if bears came to our tents. I didn't bother telling her that old Sal was getting deaf from all the shooting I'd done near her over the years.

One morning, I got up early and quietly drifted out of camp to catch some early fish. My mother arose about an hour later, peeked out of the tent and saw no boat in sight. She woke the whole camp up because she figured the boat had been swept downstream and we were all stranded. I got an ear full when I arrived back in camp.

Over the next five days we saw lots of bear sign, both black and grizzly, on the sandbars and moose sign as well. Through my spotting scope, we spotted a group of mountain goat grazing on the mountain slope about a mile from our camp. There were lots of geese all along our route and the fishing was great. It was a lot of fun catching the numerous grayling with the fly rod; we could see them approach from down deep, the water was so clear.

About five miles from Old Hogum, the river becomes shallower and I had to read the water carefully as well as pick out the right channel because the river was braided with many islands. Old Hogum is just a few old derelict log buildings now but, away from the river a bit, some Indians had built newer cabins. We met these Indians and their last names were all Alexander. The older son's name was Frank and he had been out looking for moose to shoot. He had been unsuccessful so we gave him some of the bigger dolly varden fish we had caught. He had two young children and their eyes lit up when we gave them each a chocolate bar. These were Takla Lake Indians and the grandfather, David, was getting ready for the coming trapping season. I don't think these folks had seen too many white families traveling up by long boat as they wanted to take our picture, turning the tables on the tourists.

As we headed up river the fast current and rocks made travel difficult. We were trying to maneuver around a big log jam that almost blocked off the entire river when a sharp root holed the boat below the water line. A fast run to shore for a repair job and we were again on our way. We made our last camp a few miles below the confluence of the Omineca and the Omicetla River. We only made it that far with a lot of work as we had to hand line the boat around some tight spots. Our outboard was equipped with a jet unit that helped considerably.

Earlier in the trip we had passed a couple of men who were

fishing from a newer type high-powered aluminum jet boat, about twenty-two feet long, called the *River Rogue*. The boat stopped to visit us at our camp. I was surprised that such a large boat could make it that far up the river and said as much to the captain of the craft. He explained it was simply a matter of "keeping her pinned" flat out full speed over the shallows. I was skeptical about this theory as I had bumped many sharp boulders just under the surface when we came up nice and slow, and my boat only draws six inches of water at slow speed. The *River Rogue*, I noticed, when not on plane drew about two feet of water. I also smelled whiskey when our guest was talking. His partner said nothing.

After a cup of coffee, they were off again with a roar of the powerful inboard engine. That same evening we were all sitting around the fire when we heard a metallic clunk and looked up to see the *River Rogue* being poled downstream. The two men stopped again and the one fellow had a disgusted look about him. Seems his pilot zigged when he should have zagged and drove a boulder right through the intake grate of the jet unit and the metal fragments ruined the jet impeller. They now faced a 100-mile drift all the way to Williston Lake, where they had left their truck. I've heard oil and water don't mix; now I know booze and water don't mix.

Our last day on the river was spent smoking the fish we had caught; my dad, Dan, had rigged up a smoker. The kids played on the sandbar and the weather was still holding warm and sunny. It was going to be hard to leave this beautiful river. I did go back that autumn and managed to bag one of those goats we saw, but that's another story.

# On the Fort Nelson/Liard Rivers 1983

Fishing, wild country, hunting, history—the Ft. Nelson River has it all. Our trip started with a visit to Old Ft. Nelson itself. This settlement is across the river from present day Ft. Nelson. The old place is deserted now, just an old church and a few buildings, but was once an important stop for fur traders coming from the Muskwa River and Sikanni Chief River areas. The Alaska Highway bypassed the old fort and turned it into a ghost town.

Our first night's camp was at the mouth of the Snake River, wild buffalo have been seen in this area but we didn't see any. The Ft. Nelson River is muddy so we planned to do most of our fishing where the tributaries enter. The Snake was a good bet as we caught numerous pike and pickerel here. My son, Jason, who was fourteen years old at the time, had a big one on his line right up to the boat when it snapped the leader and got away with his crocodile spoon still in its mouth. The next morning we were trying the same pool again and were getting lots of action. You can imagine my son's surprise when he landed a big pike with two spoons sticking out of its mouth. Yes, it was the same fish from the day before.

At various spots along the Ft. Nelson are old log cabins from

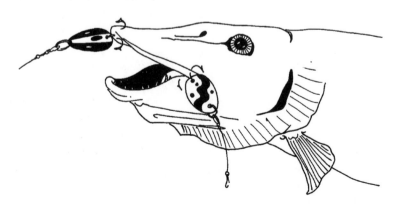

yesteryear. We would stop and poke around these sites. There is not much traffic on the river nowadays but we did see and talk to a few Sikanni Indians. Bears are numerous and we saw several grazing on the banks. Not far from Nelson Forks we passed some scenic sandstone cliffs. These cliffs had been cut out and shaped by wind and water over the centuries. Here we filled our water jugs from a clear waterfall that fell over the cliffs.

Nelson Forks, where the Ft. Nelson meets the great Liard River, was another fur trading post. There is only one abandoned cabin at this site today. The Liard is a powerful river and much clearer than the Ft. Nelson. On almost every major sweep of the Liard you can see large areas where the ice has flattened the surrounding trees at spring breakup.

I could feel the river's power as the big boils shifted our boat slightly back and forth. The old trappers must have had to be careful in their light birch bark canoes on this river. The wind has a chance to gain momentum on the wide Liard and this creates sand storms coming off the big sandbars. The Liard or "river of cottonwoods" is aptly named. There are lots of good camping spots on big bars all with a backdrop of great cottonwood trees.

We camped at the mouth of the Duneedin River about three miles up from Nelson Forks. Around 3:00 P.M. the sky began to blacken. We had heard of the thunder storms that came out of the northern Rockies and traveled down the Liard. We weren't disappointed. I didn't know it could rain so hard. The smaller of our two tents blew over and a sleeping bag got soaked. The storm was over in fifteen minutes and the sun picked up our spirits.

The next morning we headed downstream again, passing numerous large islands with the river splitting into several channels in places. I noticed a section of rougher water coming up, just a few four-foot high rollers created by some underwater boulders. I could have easily stayed to the flat water on either side of the rapid. So far this trip was all relatively smooth water. It was hot and as I looked up the boat I could see most of the crew were relaxing with their backs to the wind; my mom and two of the kids were sleeping. My wife had her head down, writing in her daily journal. I gently steered for the rollers so no one would notice. Well, you should have seen that drowsy crew come to life all at once when the boat began to buck and pound as I took her right up the middle.

We camped that afternoon on another of the Liard's beautiful bars just a few miles upstream from Ft. Liard. We had some visitors that evening, Steve Cotache and family, Natives from Ft. Liard. The Indians head up river, to where the Beaver River enters, and hunt moose on this Yukon River. The north has changed a lot for the Indians and mostly for the better. Steve's wife was pregnant and soon the Northwest Territories government would fly her out to Yellowknife to have her baby safely in the modern hospital there.

The women were starting to prepare supper and dad and I were lounging with "sundowners" in our hands when we began to hear a motor but no boat was in sight. This outboard noise continued while we ate supper and about an hour later a long riverboat appeared about a half-mile downstream from our camp. It took another forty-five minutes to pass us and go out of sight. The thirty-foot boat had three Indians in it with lots of gear and gas barrels. The current on the Liard is strong, probably five miles per hour. Talk about underpowered, with the motor screaming flat out a person on shore had to look close to see if that boat was moving at all. It was going to be a long thirty miles to the Beaver for these guys.

The old-fashioned riverboat is still king at Ft. Liard. There must have been twenty boats tied up along the river when we pulled in. This small town sits on the Liard near the mouth of the Petitot River. The local RCMP constable gave our family a tour of the town including the community center, the Hudson's Bay Store, the Liard Hotel and the Roman Catholic Church where Father Murray resides. He has been the preacher there for twenty-seven years. He also travels down by riverboat to Nahanni Butte (about eighty residents) to preach. Both the priest and the RCMP are concerned about the road scheduled to open from Ft. Nelson to Ft. Liard in 1984 because it will bring easier access to liquor with all its social problems for the Indians.

The Liard is a big river in big country and we only saw a small portion of it. I'll be going back one day again to camp on those great sandbars and see those cottonwood trees.

# On the Finlay 1990

Finally the Finlay. It had been this river with its history of riverboats and the men that ran them, some of whom I knew, that lured me to the north's rivers. Nine years after I built my boat I was at last on the waters that I named my boat for. I had wanted to run this river almost from the beginning but until now it was not feasible because of log debris from the damming that resulted in Williston Lake. The lower Finlay was drowned by the big lake's water and great rafts of logs, sometimes miles across, choked the river mouth for most of the early years of the lake's existence. These rafts could trap a boat or worse yet make it impossible to get to the shore when bad winds blew up.

Things had changed dramatically by 1990. B.C. Hydro had worked for the past twenty years on the flotsam; salvaging what they could and burning the rest on shore. What remained became waterlogged and sank. Oh, the shores still had a lot of logs on the beach and there were floating deadheads that had to be avoided as we headed up the lake from Ingenika, but it wasn't dangerous. As the lake petered out at the lake's north end, the river current could be felt and we saw a big black bear looking at us from the shore. We managed to get some good pictures.

We were now in Deserters Canyon where the worst rapids could once be found and many a boat was lost. The canyon today is under about eight feet of water so only the cliffs surrounding us give a clue as to the force the rapids must have had. It was here that two of Black's men deserted after being scared by the rapids in about 1820. Black was the earliest explorer on the Finlay and the incident gave the rapids their name.

"Holy!" my son Jason shouted as his light rod almost bent in half. A few minutes later he landed an eight-pound dolly varden. We were fishing right in the canyon near a feeder stream. Soon, three more were caught including a one-pound rainbow trout.

When the strikes dropped off, we carried on up river to the mouth of the Pesika River and made camp on a sandy bar. When the tents were all set up, my dad and I sat back with our traditional "sundowner" while my wife, Jo-Eane, and my mom, Pauline, fried up some moose steak for supper. Oh, it's a tough life.

Day three found us motoring on up river and I was having a hard time finding the right channel in this section. The river braided into many smaller streams and many didn't have deep enough water to float my boat. When the best channel was found, I had to keep a mental note where it rejoined the main current for the journey home. The Finlay is a good-size river and the biggest tributary entering the Williston Lake system. Tall mountains surrounded us and many were still snow-capped this July day.

We enjoyed six more days on the beautiful river, with our last camp just across the river from Dell Creek. Here and further up at Russell Creek we caught five dollies that weighed over twenty pounds each; the biggest fish I've ever caught. We saw three other riverboats while we were there, operated by the Ft. Ware Indians. One boatload stopped at our camp one evening when I held up the coffee pot. The three fellows were hunting moose (in July?). I asked them how they kept the meat in this heat but they didn't seem too concerned.

We saw many moose on our trip, a few bears, and the fishing was excellent. At one point, we saw two moose enter the river and, as they swam the river ahead of us, we took some good footage with our movie camera. Unwanted wildlife was also present and these mosquitoes drove us to bed early most nights.

The Finlay River was all I hoped it would be and more.

# On the Stikine 1992

"Warning! Unnavigable rapids downstream! Extreme danger!" These were the words on the sign that greeted us as we launched our riverboats into the fast moving Stikine River. We were going upstream but I felt the devil in me and almost shut off the outboard as we headed out onto the river, just to see what reaction I could get out of my wife.

Our launch point for this trip was where the Stewart-Cassiar Highway crosses the Stikine. Our destination was Highland Post, 130 miles up river. This was the fastest waterway I had ever been on. The river is always in a hurry and long calm stretches are almost nonexistent. Our boat was carrying about 4,000 pounds of gear, gas, and grub, including our family of seven people. We weren't breaking any speed records going against this strong current. We did have company on this trip. Dave and Lorraine Solomonson were traveling with us, using their own twenty-foot riverboat. Dave had guided on the upper Stikine and Spatsizi Rivers for the late Tommy Walker back in the early 1970s and this was his first trip back into the country. It was nice to have Dave's color-commentary on the country that he knew so well.

Our first camp was just below the mouth of the Klappan River and the kids enjoyed the beach and the fishing here. That evening I decided to run up with the boat to look over the rapids at Goat Canyon. Beggarly Creek enters at this point just after the river makes a 90° bend. The water here is swift with high standing waves. To complicate matters, a big rock projection juts out into the current and behind this a great whirlpool forms. The river was fairly low so that was in our favor.

The next day, to be on the safe side, I decided to bring the gas up above the rapids on one trip and the family and gear up on the next. Things went smoothly and the kids enjoyed the exhilarating ride through the canyon.

To give the reader an idea of the force of the water in the canyon, I offer the following story. A few years earlier two men in an eighteen-foot riverboat ran this rapid. They were powered by a ninety horsepower outboard. There had been considerable rain in the mountains and the canyon water level was up some eight feet in a matter of three days from its low point. The men were endeavoring to power their way up. To avoid the big whirlpool with its deep vortex and stay out of the ten foot standing haystacks of waves, they had to hug the whirlpool's outer edge. Traveling at about fifteen mph, their motor screaming, they just entered the chosen path when the whirlpool spun the boat around in a flash and they were headed back downstream. This was repeated twice more before the men barely made it through. After bailing out the boat and changing their underwear, they were again on their way.

On this morning, our third, the air was thick with smoke from a forest fire somewhere up ahead. A park warden, on his way back from the Spatsizi country, pulled his boat beside ours to give us the latest update on the fire. It was burning now on both banks of the river, having jumped the river a few days earlier. We would be in the midst of it eight miles up stream. Fire is a natural phenomenon in the Park so no effort was being made to put it out. As we entered the section of river where the fire was burning, trees were flaring up on either side of us and we got some great footage of the fire on the video tape recorder.

Our camp above the Pitman River was our best for fishing yet. Our twin girls, Marilyn and Michelle, caught some nice dolly varden right from the bank. We saw moose and bear on the banks and on a high cliff over the river was a big mountain goat.

August 13, a frosty morning, saw us on our way to the Spatsizi River. This is a clear river with great surrounding mountain scenery. We arrived at Highland Post at 3:00 P.M. This was once a fur trading post that traded with the Indians who lived in the country. The Indians have long ago gone to live by the highways closer to civilization. The Post now belongs to Ray Collingwood, a big game outfitter. I'd met and known Ray in the past and he kindly gave us permission to use his cabins. It was great to get cleaned up with a shower and stay in something other than a tent for a few days. While in Highland Post we climbed up to the plateau, for a firsthand view of this great game country.

On our way back down the Stikine we had to negotiate Jewel Canyon. Coming upstream had been no problem but going down was tricky. The river here runs through a mine field of car-size boulders for a good mile. Many canoes have been lost here when their backs were broken on a rock. I made it through with no problems, but Dave had to travel faster than I did to keep up on plane in his boat. He was almost at the end when he hit hard on a rock. After inspection, it was obvious no real damage occurred.

Downstream a few miles it was my turn to hit. The river shallowed out for 300 yards as it approached a rift, or lip of gravel, which cut across at an angle. The water spilled over this lip in four places with the steep chute ending up against a cliff face. Dave made it down ahead of me and could turn his shorter boat downstream before hitting the rock wall. My longer boat (thirty-six feet) didn't make it. We went over the fall as slow as possible but shot straight ahead and the bow hit the face square on. I think every weld in my boat was tested as well as my back fillings when we hit. Luckily no damage resulted so I guess I'm not that bad an aluminum welder after all.

The Stikine is not a river for beginners. As my son said, "it's not a hands-in-your-pockets river for the captain." I love the country of the Spatsizi and its abundant wildlife. The park status ensures the river and country around it will always be there for the adventurer.

# On the Kechika 1994

This year we explored the Kechika River—the land of stone sheep, elk, goats, moose, deer and bear. The northern limits of the Rocky Mountains were the backdrop as we traveled the Kechika River upstream from where it empties into the Liard River. No roads or railways border this river valley; we were in wilderness. It was a wonderful feeling to be piloting my river-boat on this waterway for the first time.

Our friends, Dave and Lorraine Solomonson, joined us, using their own boat. Mechanical breakdowns are always a possibility on these trips and a backup boat can be an ace in the hole. We were no sooner underway when a spark plug fouled on my out-board. Dave turned his boat around to see what the trouble was and got stuck on a sandbar. I had to pull him off with my boat when I got it running again.

Our first bivouac was at the mouth of the Red River, really just a creek in August. The fishing there was excellent for both pike and dolly varden. We ate fish for supper that night and by morning the haze of a distant forest fire was moving up the valley; we found out later it started in the Northwest Territories.

"What's that swimming ahead of us?" someone asked. The swimmers turned out to be a sow black bear with twin cubs. They beached just ahead of us and couldn't have picked a worse spot for them and a better spot for us. The banks here were 100 feet of steep clay slope. The bears had to traverse this slide because it was too steep to climb and we were able to get some good photos of them.

The weather had been sunny and hot for the past four days and the nights were clear. We had been getting lazy with our camp and hadn't bothered setting up the heavy canvas fly over our tent. Around 2:00 A.M., the flashes were lighting up our tent but the delayed thunder indicated the storm was still a long way off. "Maybe it will miss us," I thought, with my wife and children sleeping soundly. Boom! The whole tent shook; that was close and next came the rain and wind. Everybody was up, using flashlights and lightning to see by, to help tarp down the camp in the driving rain. For two hours the storm lashed at us and only let up just before dawn.

The sun was again shining as we made our way up stream to the meeting of the Turnagain River. Here we did a little fishing while the kids climbed a small hill to run off some steam. This Kechika country looks fairly dry and the big game guides here claim they can winter over their pack horses without putting up any hay for them, as the low snowfall allows the animals to paw down to cured grass. We noticed two varieties of low junipers and wild potentilla were blooming. On the hillside was a low form of sagebrush and wild onions were abundant.

The Kechika is a muddy river, more so when there are big rains in the upper valley. We fished the clear stream mouths and got our drinking water from the same source. Our camp at the mouth of Denitiah Creek was a beauty for scenery as the mountains here are close to the main river. I dug out my spotting scope

from the duffle and in the evening put it to use. In a short time I located a herd of stone sheep, about sixteen in all. They were feeding on a green slope well above timberline. Nine mountain goats were also feeding 200 yards below the sheep. All the children took turns looking through the scope.

Wednesday, August 10, we were up at 7:00 A.M. and noticed two different float planes overhead. No doubt these were servicing the outfitter's camp at Terminus Mountain. Big game guiding season would soon be here. Canada geese were also on the move and several flocks flew past us as we ate breakfast. This day we traveled to the junction of the Gataga and Kechika Rivers. The Gataga turned out to be a dirty river; once we passed it, the Kechika was clear as glass and here would be our last camp. Brownie Mountain was our sentinel at this camp and the fishing did not disappoint us. The kids caught four dollies for supper.

The following day we headed up river to where the Frog River entered. This was actually the bigger of the two rivers, so we traveled up it for a few miles to try our luck fishing. My sons, Henry and Bernard Jr., both caught some nice fish, while a buck mule deer, antlers still in velvet, was watching. We returned that afternoon to our camp on the Kechika and the wives cooked up a big pot of homemade beans and baked bread for supper while Dave and I had our "sundowner."

The trip back down river was noteworthy as we saw several moose and bears. On a small ledge about ten feet from the river we came across a big, male mountain goat. It is unusual to find his kind this far down from the safety of the mountains. He no doubt was a goat in search of new country. He was wet and must have just swum the river. He stamped his front foot at us as I swung the boat in close to him for a picture.

The last ten miles or so of the Kechika, before it meets the Liard, has many sets of rapids. The river has to cut itself down to the level of the bigger river. In several places we got wet from big waves smacking the bow. These rapids are no trouble for a riverboat but a canoeist would want to pick his routes carefully. Again we were back at the Liard River and civilization: the Alaska Highway.

# Buck Fever—Grizzly Style

If a hunter wants to shoot straight, he couldn't pick a better time to do so than when drawing down on a grizzly. This is one animal that can make a flincher out of a dead man. It may have something to do with the fact a grizzly has been known to bite back, or perhaps it's all the hype that's been written over the years about how dangerous a grizzly is, especially when wounded. It is a wise guide that keeps this all in mind when guiding a hunter into shooting range of the big bear.

My hunter for ten days was a twenty-six-year old, strapping six-foot four-inch policeman from Susanville, California. Mark was on the police "swat" team for his area of northern California and prided himself on his shooting ability and with good reason. These special teams had to be able to group their shots to a nickel at 100 yards or they wouldn't make the team. I felt confident that if Mark could put a bullet into a felon's temple even if the man had his arm around a hysterical hostage, he should do just fine on a 500-pound grizzly. His dad would accompany us, but he was only tagged out for a black bear.

We had flown into a remote lake north of Smithers where the bear hunting was good. The mountains across the lake were steep and, during the winter, snow slides had kept the sloping draws bare of snow. These draws were the first areas to green up in the spring and they attracted the hungry bears that had just come out of hibernation.

We arrived on June 1 and our expectations were high. One problem, though, the lake was still partially frozen on the far side. Sure enough, that afternoon we spotted a bear but couldn't break through the ice with the boat. It was too far to walk around the lake, not to mention that there was still three feet of snow in the shade under the trees on our side.

For three days we were stuck on our side of the lake. Talk

about maddening; every day we saw bear and once saw three spread out over the mountain. Finally the third night was stormy with lots of wind and we awoke to a wide-open lake but no bears in sight.

Midday found us glassing the slopes again and Mark spotted a bear. I put the spotting scope on the bear and he looked good. Let's go! We piled into the boat for the three-quarter mile trip to the other side and the base of the mountain. We beached the boat and started the climb up to where we last saw the bear. An hour of huffing and puffing and we had reached timberline. The bear was not in sight. We spent about two hours looking, hoping he might just have dropped into one of the many dips in the face of the mountain. It's funny how flat a mountain face looks when viewed from afar, but once you're on it, it's a different story.

Either the bear winded us, heard us or just plain wandered off; one thing for sure, he wasn't here. Back to camp we went. Mark's dad was more disappointed than we were, as he had lugged his movie camera all the way up to get the action on film. He was no spring chicken and the climb took a lot out of him. Oh well, tomorrow would be another day and what a day it turned out to be.

One hour after sunrise we spotted him, a big bear, a keeper. He was on the move and we hoped he would settle down and feed, so we would have a better chance to stalk him. The bear was going to cross our trail from yesterday. When he came to it, it was as if he hit a wall. He stood up, sniffed the air, dropped to all fours and ran for the timber. Coffee anybody?

We passed the high noon mark on the clock and at about 1:00 P.M. a bear appeared, not as big as the morning bear but this one had a beautiful coat. His back was silver tipped to halfway down the side. The best part was that it had found a nice patch of green that we figured would hold him all afternoon. We fired up the kicker on the twenty-four-foot riverboat and were off.

We made our climb up in about three-quarters of an hour but when we left the last of the timber it was a repeat of yesterday, no bear. This time we kept climbing because I thought the added elevation might give us a better view. After a while, I told Mark to stay with his dad, as he was played out, and I would go up

another 100 yards to a rock outcrop and look around. There was a small ravine about thirty yards from me that ran up the mountain. On the far side of this were patches of ground balsam bent over from the avalanches. On the edge of one of these patches was an upturned stump. I got myself comfortable and started to glass this area of green. I passed over the stump several times with my glasses, but about the third pass the "stump" lifted its head. Our grizzly! The bear laid his head back down and went back to his slumber. I waved Mark up to my location. When he arrived he asked if I had seen anything and I pointed out the "stump" about ninety yards away. "That's our bear," I said. "Looks like a root to me," Mark said. "You just wait and he'll move again," I predicted. We waited about ten minutes and I could see Mark was skeptical.

The bear stood up. I could see the excitement in Mark's face. He got himself a rest on a small tree and took aim with his .300 Weatherby Magnum. Boom! The bear swapped ends and I could see gravel fly at his feet. "Where did I hit him?" Mark asked. "You didn't," I said. "I couldn't have missed!" Mark said as he chambered another round. This time he didn't miss and the bear was bowled over. The bear lay still for a second and then kicked out with his legs and began to roll. Down the hill he rolled, ass over tea kettle. His trajectory carried him past Mark's dad who took a Hail Mary shot from the hip as the bear rolled past him. The bruin finally came to rest on some loose shale about 300 yards below us. We hurried down the slope. Our bear was a 400-pound dry sow. Not a bad size for a female mountain grizzly. After the necessary photo session, I skinned her out. While I was working, Mark was commenting to his dad about how tough grizzlies are as this one took his first bullet without going down. I said nothing. After the hide was off, we examined the bear; there was only one hole. Mark now finally realized that his first shot was a clear miss. "What am I going to tell my buddies back home?" he asked. "Tell them you shot your first bullet into the air to give the bear a sporting chance," I joked.

Both hunters had a good time and Mark's dad even got a black bear. I now know even the best shooters can get the shakes when it comes to grizzly hunting.

# Blood Lust

There was no mistaking the sign. The snow had been flattened all around by hooves and padded feet. Great chunks of moose hair mixed with blood stained the snow. It was 8:00 A.M., just breaking day as I pulled up in my skidoo. No sign of the combatants could be seen. They likely took off when they heard me approach. Moose tracks led to the heavy timber. I could have followed but this time I didn't bother as I knew what I would find. Yes, the moose would still be alive; he might not even look too bad. I'd seen this act played out many times over my years of trapping. The wolves hounded the moose out to an open spot and, circling it, took turns lunging at its hind quarters. They don't actually hamstring it, but inflict vise-hard bites to the upper back legs. The moose's adrenalin is pumping and he fights back the best he can against bad odds. He doesn't feel much pain from these muscle wounds, yet. At this point the pack usually pulls away and calmly waits.

A patient animal the wolf; they know the moose will only run a short distance and rest. A few hours later and the moose begins to stiffen up. I had to leave to continue my rounds; I still had lots of traps to check. The wolves would be back in the evening and they'd find the moose so stiff and sore he'd be defenseless. They may kill him right away or just as often they'll just pull him down and begin to eat while he is still alive—a grim business.

Wolf attacks sometimes follow a different script. One spring day I was walking around the shore of a small lake in old growth timber along a good moose trail. Patches of moose hair began to show up on the trail. I carried on and the hair chunks became bigger. Halfway around the lake, about one-quarter mile from the first hair sign, lay the partially eaten moose, a young cow. It's a common practice for wolves to pick out the younger animals. An old cow or bull would have had enough smarts to run into the lake and swim for the far shore and safety. This cow had panicked and just kept running while the pack pulled her apart piece by piece.

It was cold, about -30°C., when I bounced out of the timbered trail on my Tundra skidoo onto Terrapin Lake. Off to my left, standing out on the lake, were a cow and calf moose and both animals were covered by hoarfrost around their chests and heads. The cow's hackles were standing up so I passed them in a wide arc. It was then that I noticed the wolf tracks all around the ice. That explained the frost. These two had put in a tough night. The cow had been fighting for her calf's life and was in an ugly mood this morning. I wished the old girl luck and continued on my rounds.

Two days later I was back and there was the calf strung out in pieces along the lakeshore. There was no sign of the cow. She had lost that valiant fight and left. I believe when a pack of wolves gets a calf in their sights, it is doomed; sooner or later the cow lets her guard down and it's all over.

In early May of 1982, I was exploring for new beaver colonies and had walked into a small, wet meadow. As I circled, just at the edge, I noticed something white that looked unnatural poking up from the grass about 100 feet ahead. It was the rib cage of a large moose. I looked closer and discovered the remains of two large bull moose that had been fighting the previous fall. They had locked antlers! It was a lucky group of wolves that came on this scene. Most of the bones were gone but the shoulder or front blade bones of both moose as well as the rib cage remained. Wolves always leave these shoulder blade bones as there is no marrow in them. Both skulls and antlers were still locked. I couldn't get them apart so I dragged them into the bush and wired them four feet up a tree. The following spring I went back with a trapper nelson (pack frame). By now the antlers had shrunk a little and I managed to pry them apart. I packed the biggest rack home and it now hangs over one of my cabins, skull and all, at Hoodoo Lake.

Contrary to the ramblings of the various nature shows on television, the wolf sometimes kills purely for sport. Most trappers have seen the carnage that occurs when March comes with a good crust on four or five feet of snow. This is the time for the wolves to have fun. They can scamper across the top of the snow while the poor unfortunate moose flounders along, sinking chest deep. The moose is already weak from putting in a tough winter, maybe has a pretty good load of blood sucking ticks on his body, and the cows are usually heavy with calf. When this situation exists, the wolves kill far more than they could possibly eat. I've seen only the entrails and the fetus eaten; the rest is left for the ravens.

One morning in March of 1991, I spotted a lone wolf approaching my home at Hoodoo Lake. He was traveling across the lake ice toward the home corral. I loaded up my .270 Winchester and stepped out on the porch. The wolf heard me, I guess, and trotted off out of range.

My neighbor, Eric Rahn, and his wife had enjoyed watching a cow moose feeding a few yards from their house for the past week. A day after I saw the wolf, Eric noticed the moose was gone. He looked around and found the body near by. Nothing had been eaten. The moose's nose had been torn off but no other

injuries were evident. From the blood on the snow and the tracks, Eric pieced together what had happened. A lone wolf is usually a tougher customer than the average; he has to be to survive alone. This wolf had clamped onto the moose's nose and no amount of shaking could dislodge the wolf until the nose tore off. The moose then blew blood in a circle all around her until she slowly died—a rough way to go.

"Look at the dogs out on the lake, Dad," my daughter Marilyn said. I took one look at the six wolves and grabbed my rifle. I had a young stud colt I was boarding in the corral for a neighbor and the wolves were heading in that direction. I fired at the leader of the pack and at the shot the entire pack bolted for the bush. I put on my coat and snowshoes and walked out onto the ice to where the leader had stood when I shot. A short distance into the bush I found the dead animal.

The wolf is not the only bad customer the moose has to deal with. The black bear also likes to get into the act. A great opportunist is the black bear. I had been cutting trail to a lake one June day when I smelled rotten meat. As I cautiously approached the lake edge, there ahead of me were two bears looking back at me. Both walked off a few steps and then ran for cover. They were working on a half-eaten moose. It was easy to see what happened. The beaver had brushed out a good trail to the lake edge and it was the only clear landing site around. I figured the moose was swimming the lake and the two bears happened to be where the unlucky moose decided to beach. They no doubt saw and heard her from afar and simply waited. There was a slight incline on the beaver run, up from the water, with big spruce trees on both sides of the trail; perfect for an ambush. The moose must have been cold-cocked with one mighty blow to the head as she climbed out of the water; it appeared she had a broken neck.

Bears sometimes kill moose calves in the spring of the year. They seem to like only the hind hams and often only two holes are eaten into each hind quarter. My wife and I had been watching a cow and newborn calf moose one afternoon and later discovered the calf with one hind leg caught in the barbed wire fence that runs along our field. Sure enough, only the two hams had been eaten out. This was likely a small bear for he didn't even remove the calf from the fence, but just ate from the calf right where he was.

Most poultry farmers know how a weasel will kill every chicken in the coop. The weasel's blood is up and he just can't help himself. He kills for the sport and only stops when all motion ceases. A fox has been known to do the same. The worst case of wanton slaughter I have ever heard of happened twenty years ago up near Tatlatui Park. I've guided in this area and know it well. Each range of mountains has its resident herd of mountain goats. The goats on one particular drainage just disappeared. The Ministry of Environment investigated along with the outfitter in the area and discovered the culprit—wolf. From the large number of skeletal remains the experts pieced together the events.

Goats periodically change ranges and often must descend to the valley to do so. This herd of thirty goats, mostly nannies and kids, had descended to the valley when a pack of wolves intercepted them. The goats were caught cold turkey in a narrow stream bed and were systematically killed, one after another, until not one survived. From the large number of bones at the site, most of the meat was used by the ravens as wolves tend to pack large portions away to eat. It took almost to the present time for the goats in the surrounding country to repopulate this range.

# Black Powder Moose

In the fall of 1994, my client was Scott Glanville from Washington. He had never hunted moose before. Now Scott was not a man who stretched the truth and when he said he could kill a moose with his .50 caliber black powder rifle I did not doubt him. After all, I had seen him shoot a running black bear the previous spring and kill it with one shot!

Using a black powder rifle to hunt big game is becoming more popular with hunters in North America today. This kind of weapon was in widespread use until the turn of the century when more modern rifles, using smokeless powder cartridges, were invented. The black powder rifle fires only one shot and then must be reloaded, a process that can take several minutes. As the name implies, black powder is used as the propellant. A measured load of black powder is poured into the muzzle and a lead ball patched with cloth is pushed down the barrel. A small percussion cap is then placed on a nipple under the hammer. When the hammer falls, driving sparks into the load, the rifle fires and a considerable amount of smoke is discharged along with the bullet. The range of the weapon is considerably less than a modern hunting rifle, rarely exceeding 100 yards. Hunting is a purist's sport and many people enjoy using the older-style weapons.

The rut was in full swing when Scott, his partner Mike Leiser, and I began hunting. Mike was from Portland, Oregon, and had missed his chance at a bear earlier in this hunt. Now it was Scott's turn to shoot. We had hunted for three days, walking into many lakes and swamps. We had seen a lot of moose sign including tracks and peeled saplings where the bulls had rubbed the velvet off their antlers. In one wet spot I showed the men a moose wallow. This is where the bull digs up the ground with his hooves. He then urinates in this dirt hole and rolls around in it until he smells "sweet" for his mate. We were doing everything right but the moose were not cooperating; we had seen nothing.

On the afternoon of September 27 we hiked into a small lake where I had seen moose sign earlier in the season. We had about a mile hike to the lake, a lake typical of many good moose lakes in the central interior of B.C., with a good deal of willows and swamp around the edges. "Ungh, Ungh." No mistaking that sound—a bull moose. We were still 100 feet from the lake, in the heavy timber, when we first heard it. As we cautiously stepped out on a small point of land, we saw at the end of the lake a cow and calf moose. "Where's the bull?" asked Scott. "He'll be just inside the timber," I said, and when the cow had finished her drink and stepped into the bush with her calf at heel, out stepped the bull. And what a bull! Even at 400 yards we didn't need binoculars to see his great set of antlers. Scott followed me as I stepped back into the timber to move closer to the moose and cut down the distance to within range of Scott's primitive weapon. At 200 yards I looked at Scott and he whispered he wanted to give it a try. This would be just about the limit of his rifle's range. It was necessary to step into the water to get a clear shot at the unsuspecting moose. Scott found a deadfall to use as a rest and let off a shot. Through the smoke I could see the ball hit the water in front of the moose. "Too low," I said. Scott hurried to shore and began to reload, a procedure that took at least a minute. Stepping back in the water, Scott shot and this time I did not see where the shot hit. The moose, showing no reaction, began to move back to the heavy timber. Before Scott could reload, the bull disappeared in the woods.

Scott looked disappointed but I heard the bull still calling and I figured if we moved in his direction and did a little grunting ourselves, we might get another chance. We were still fifty yards away from where we last saw the moose when the sound of branches cracking told us the moose was coming our way. I told Scott to get ready as this guy was coming right for us. I called again and the bull burst from the willows into the shallow water and came running at us. "Shoot!" I said, and at thirty feet Scott put a bullet into his neck. The bull's momentum carried him about another ten feet and he went down with a splash. His death throes carried him into deep water and I was afraid he might sink.

When all motion stopped, only a small patch of belly hide showed where the moose was. Now the work started—with me taking a cold dip in the lake. When we finally got him to shore, I held up his head as best as I could and Scott took a few photos and a quick point count. This was a dandy moose with twenty-one points and a fifty-inch spread. Not bad for his first moose.

I sent Scott back to get the pack with my meat saw in it. I had left it where he first shot at the moose. While he was gone, I worked strictly by feel to gut the moose in the water. My teeth were chattering after twenty minutes in the chest-deep water. I was out of the water and drying off when Scott returned. "What took you so long?" I asked. It turns out another bull moose had heard all the calling going on and had come to join the battle. As Scott was returning with my backpack he almost ran into this new bull on the trail. The moose stood his ground and wouldn't let him pass. Scott hadn't bothered reloading his rifle and was pretty nervous as he waited for the big animal to move off.

We spent the next day packing out the meat with my pack horses. I weighed the hanging quarters with my beam scale back home at Hoodoo Lake and they totaled 810 pounds. From this I would estimate the bull's live weight to be approximately 1,600 pounds. His antlers alone weighed forty-five pounds and green scored seventh place in the Boone & Crockett records for moose taken with black powder rifles.

# Lady Luck

If there is a drawback to the guiding business it's that often I don't have much time to hunt my own moose. I was busy in the fall of 1994, with clients arriving in early September and the last hunters not leaving until October 24. My time for hunting was running short, as the season in our area closes November 3.

I'd spent about three days hunting for a bull moose, any bull moose, because this year I had lucked out on the limited entry draw. Nothing with antlers was my lot so far. The weather was holding fair so I asked my wife Jo-Eane to accompany me for a day's hunting and maybe a change of luck.

Our destination was a dry meadow of about forty acres in size. I had seen lots of sign in this area, especially beds. I figured my wife could handle the two-mile hike from the logging road to this spot. I had been here twice before this season and had seen a big grizzly on the second trip, but no moose. I was hoping there would be no sign of the grizzly this time because it was not likely any moose would be hanging around if he was still about.

It took about one and a half hours to reach the meadow, hunting as we went. I had just shown my wife the spot where the big bear had been. Glassing the far side for moose, I could see a dead tree sticking out from the bank about four feet off the ground and 400 yards away. Some distance behind this was a stump covered with frost. We then went on. After another fifty yards or so, I again looked at the frosty stump through the binoculars and, lo and behold, it moved. The grizzly again? No, I could see antlers moving.

"Moose," I said to my wife, "a big bull. Let's get a closer look." We cut the distance down to about 350 yards and I left Jo-Eane at a small grove of trees that grew in the meadow. I gave her my binoculars and said I wanted to get closer before taking a shot, but I didn't get far. A small, deep creek cut straight across in front of me, right across the meadow. I backtracked to the small grove of trees as that was the only place I could get a rest. "It's too far away," my wife said.

I figured if I arranged a good rest by lopping off a few branches from a nearby tree, I could get off a good steady shot. My .270 rifle barked—no reaction from the moose. I shot again, this time raising the cross-hairs just above the moose's back. Still no reaction. I held two feet over his back and squeezed off a third shot. The moose jumped, ran in a circle and stood facing me. I held over his head and shot again—nothing. I knew I had jerked the trigger on this one. On my next shot Jo-Eane said "You got him." She was watching the action through the binoculars and saw the moose fall.

It took about a half-hour to get around the creek and up to where I'd last seen the moose. I spotted the antlers first, sticking up over the willows. This was a big bull in his prime and there would be no problem feeding the family this year.

The following day was spent packing the meat out with the help of my three sons and three pack horses. It took us nine hours to get the job done. The going was tough for the horses in the spongy ground. We also took out the antlers, a nice set for this area. They measured forty-seven inches across and had heavy main beams. I guess I'll have to bring my wife along more often.

# Laugh While You're Hunting

A good sense of humor is a real asset around a hunting camp. Four Washington State hunters and I had just flown into our camp on Muskeg Lake. My boss, Art Bracey, was there to pick us up with his riverboat. By the time we unloaded the duffle it was noon, so we headed into the cook shack for lunch. Later, one hunter (we'll call him Harold) stepped outside for fresh air and saw a moose far down the lakeshore. "Hey! There's a moose!" he shouted, and we all piled outside to look. Sure enough it was a big cow. These guys were after meat, so Art and I headed for the boat while Harold and another hunter got their rifles ready. With me at the stern and the two hunters aboard, Art shoved off from shore and jumped aboard—well almost. He fell in the thick muck near shore, face first. We got him pulled out. I then changed places with the "bog man" and we were off.

The patient moose was just standing on the beach as Art killed the motor. Harold rested his rifle on the boat's front deck and got ready to shoot. At the shot there was an explosion of wood chips as the bow was shot out. Pieces of plywood rained down around us. "A little higher Harold," Art said sarcastically. We were cracking up with laughter.

On another trip my client was a hunter named Ray. He was a good hunter who liked a joke even if the laugh was at his expense. Ray's equipment was usually the best money could buy, and I'd told him by letter to bring along some hip waders and good hiking boots for our coming fall hunt. When he arrived he proudly showed me his new Gore-Tex hiking boots with the soft rubber soles. Excellent for traction, he assured me.

We were to hunt moose on the river for the first few days. I was surprised to see Ray pull out cheap plastic throw away chest waders. "No sense buying good chest waders for just one time use," he said, "These pull right over your regular boots." I watched as he put his first leg in. The second leg went in and his boot tore right out the bottom. "Well, one dry leg is better than none," I said, with a smirk on my face. We walked the canoe into deeper water and I held the gunwale while Ray climbed in. Rip! There went the backside out of what was left of the waders. Undaunted, we headed up river.

Three hours later we were in my small cabin with a good fire going and Ray's clothes hung up to dry. His new hiking boots were soaked through so they were set on a short firelog to dry in front of my barrel heater. We had been swapping lies over coffee for about an hour when I began to smell something burning. I looked over and saw the soles on his new boots melting and hanging like icicles onto the floor. Ray quickly poured water on them and surveyed the damage. Ray and I had made a pair of "slicks" out of his $200 boots.

Yet another time, my hunter, Bill, had missed three pretty good chances at black bears in six days. He was jerking the trigger; we both knew it and he admitted he was too excited. The seventh and last day came and sure enough, two hours from camp a dandy bear was standing 120 yards ahead of us. The shot, the miss, and his hunt was over for the year. I didn't dare laugh but Bill did. "Boy! Did that bear ever run!" Bill said. I got a letter from him later that same fall saying he would be back the following spring for another try. "I'm bringing a spear up with me this time," Bill wrote, "that way I won't scare so many bears."

Buck fever can make a man do strange things. A colleague of mine once had an excitable chap in camp who had not scored on a moose yet, even though it was his second trip to B.C. and there had been several opportunities. His chance came toward the end of the week's hunt in the form of a bull moose at seventy yards. He raised his rifle, shouted "bang!" and ejected the unfired round and repeated the process until he emptied his clip. When the moose didn't fall he turned excitedly to his guide and asked, "Did I get him?" "No, you haven't shot yet," said the guide as he held in the palm of his hand all five live rounds that he had just picked up from the ground.

Of course, a competent, skilled guide like myself never makes any mistakes; well, almost never. There was that little episode when I tied my riverboat as high as I could to a tree on the riverbank. This was springtime, but I was sure the river had peaked and although my plywood boat leaked a bit I knew everything would be fine until my return five days hence.

When I returned my boat was gone, stolen I thought at first, but then I saw my bow rope tied to the tree and discovered the boat was completely submerged by the still-rising water. My outboard motor, transistor radio and other gear were also under water. I managed to pull everything out of the water with my hand winch, but that outboard motor never did run right again.

I've been a little smug at times when others miss an easy shot at game, but when I think of the chance that I blew back in 1980, it puts me in my place. I had just posted my son Jason on a point of land that afforded a good view of the small lake we were hunting and I had moved back into the timber to watch a game trail. This trail led down to the lake and I had only been watching it for about ten minutes when I heard a twig snap. Thirty feet away was a young bull moose coming down the trail. I was completely hidden beside a big spruce tree that grew alongside the trail. I figured I'd just wait until the moose passed me by and then shoot him at point-blank range. As the moose appeared, his head was only eighteen inches from the muzzle of my rifle and I thought I'd be smart and shoot him right behind the ear. I fired too high and the bullet sailed over the moose's neck. He took off like a comet and I didn't even have time to get off another shot. That moose's ears are probably still ringing to this day. I know that occasionally mine do.

# Of Moose and Men

Discuss the moose population in the north and no two sportsmen will agree. The old timers will state emphatically "there aren't as many moose as there used to be." The newcomer, especially a neophyte hunter with limited skill, will probably side with them. Just how healthy is our moose population?

The Carrier Indians from our area had no word in their language for moose when the white man first arrived. The reason is that there were no moose in their country. When Simon Fraser and his men came, they found the Carrier Indians were mainly fish eaters, the Pacific salmon being extremely plentiful. In fact, when the fish runs failed, mass starvation was not unheard of. Yes, there were a few deer and bears in the area, but the first moose didn't show up around Prince George until the late teens and early 1920s. My neighbor, Bert Peterson, who is seventy-seven years old and has lived just north of Prince George all his life, remembers the excitement when the first moose appeared near Hoodoo Lake.

Bert, as a young lad, was playing near his father's barn and happened to look up the field to see a strange horse standing out in the grass. He ran to his Dad with the news. His father took one look and sent the boy for his rifle. He shot that moose for some much-needed meat. The neighbors from a mile away rode over by horse to see what the shooting was all about. The Petersons ended up sharing their prize with their neighbors.

Biologists generally agree that the moose migrated into the region from the north. The upper Finlay and Peace River country had always had moose. The forest fires, some deliberately set by settlers, were creating moose habitat and no vacuum exists in nature. By the 1930s the moose were thick and along with them came the wolves. Bert remembers counting thirty-four moose around the shore of Hoodoo Lake one morning in the spring of

1937. As he made his way about the trapline, he was continually pushing moose up from their beds. By the 1940s the wolves were being seen regularly, even in broad daylight. The ticks were also getting out of hand. Bert would jump a moose from its snow bed in March and the snow would be crawling with ticks and red with blood from the tick bites. Some moose would be so weakened they wouldn't make the coming of spring.

When I started moose hunting in 1968, the moose seemed to be reasonably abundant, at least to my untrained eye. There was a liberal season for both bulls and cows. The human population was also building up, however, and by the mid-1970s it was plain to see that the moose population was dropping off. The wolf population remained high to the detriment of both moose and deer. Something had to give. The biologists knew they could never hope to maintain the artificially high moose populations of the 1930s and 1940s but they also knew the moose range could feed a lot more animals than now existed, so new regulations were brought in. The season was shortened, cow moose and mature bulls could only be taken by special permit, i.e. limited entry draw, and only two-point or smaller bulls could be taken by the general hunting public. A short calf-only season was also instituted. These regulations have been in effect to the present time, almost twenty years, and my own assessment is that it has worked, albeit modestly. The biggest improvement has been the increase of bull moose. If the bull can make it past his first year and a half of life, that is survive the calf and small antler stage, his odds of living to a ripe old age are fairly good. I'm seeing a lot more big-antlered moose in my travels than I did, say, ten years ago.

The cow moose are also on the increase. Some of these animals are living to a tremendous age. In 1992, my son Bernard Jr. shot his first moose. He had been lucky enough to draw a rare cow permit and it was an excited boy when that animal hit the ground. He was proudly supplying the table meat for our family of eight for the next year. He dutifully sent in the lower tooth for aging. This was the toughest moose meat I had ever eaten. We almost mounted the grinder right on the kitchen table. I couldn't understand it. I had done the usual things. I hung the carcass up for a week to age, kept the meat clean, quick froze it after cutting and still even the gravy was tough. The answer came about three months later with the tooth aging results. That moose was eighteen years old!

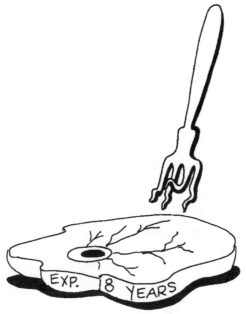

# Murphy's Law and Hunting

Bad luck plagues some hunters. I invited my cousin Dan McKay (from Long Beach, California) and his brother Tom up for a combination moose and bear hunt in 1991. Dan mentioned he had only limited success over the years hunting deer around his native state. He mostly hunted with the bow and arrow, so that in itself is a limiting factor compared to the rifle.

On our second day of a seven-day hunt, we were coming back from an unsuccessful morning moose hunt. The trail we were on was mostly clear of timber on both sides for seventy-five feet. We had just passed a grove of heavy timber when a bear appeared from the low bush, took one look at us and promptly bolted for the bush. From experience, I knew that if we continued until we were out of sight and sound of the bear, he would probably be back out to feed on the grass growing in the clearing.

We were patiently waiting about 100 yards away from the spot where the bruin disappeared, when a bear head popped out from the trees to look around. We froze. Now, bears can pick up motion out to about 200 feet pretty well, but are pathetic at picking out a motionless hunter. This bear was no exception. He proceeded out of the cover into the open, walked to an old rotten stump and started to feed on something.

We started our stalk. The breeze was in our face and every time the bear raised his head we stopped. I was leading, with Dan and Tom directly behind me so we wouldn't show a large silhouette. At about fifty yards we crouched as we walked; at thirty yards I waved Dan around in front of me. Dan slowly raised himself to full height as he pulled back his seventy-pound-pull bow. At the release I saw the arrow fly and disappear into the bear just behind the shoulder—a good hit. The bear spun around and I could see a foot of arrow sticking out of his side. He leaped into the heavy timber and was gone from sight in a flash.

An animal dies of hemorrhage or loss of blood when shot with an arrow and this may take several minutes. We sat on a log and waited about a quarter of an hour. A bear leaves a poor blood trail as anyone who has washed out a bear hide knows. The hair soaks up water (or blood) like a sponge. The area inside the timber was a nightmare of downed trees over more downed trees. We were off the ground crawling along logs as much as we were on the ground. Dan figured the bear, hit as he was, would not go more than 100 yards or so before laying down to die. He might have been right or wrong; we'll never know because we never found that bear. For six hours we searched in vain, back and forth tracing and retracing our steps. We swung in wider and wider arcs from the point of entry into the woods. I searched for traces of blood on all the blown down logs the bear must have crossed. We crisscrossed an area a quarter mile deep and the same across. No search and rescue team could have done more than we did.

Three days later we came back to see if we could spot ravens circling about as those wise old sharp eyes miss nothing. Not even the birds had found our quarry. I figure that bear must have crawled under a root or stump or perhaps into a hidden den to die. All in all, a disappointing outcome for the two hunters.

Some hunters tempt Murphy's Law in spades. It puzzles me why a guy will buy a brand new rifle when he goes on his first big game trip to Canada and leave his old reliable 30-06 at home. He may have used that rifle for twenty years, is thoroughly familiar with it and knows to within an inch where it shoots. He instinctively knows where the safety is and probably has worked up some deadly accurate hand loads for it. All this and he still thinks he needs a new big magnum to do the job on moose.

My hunter from Mississippi had a slick new rifle. It was a nylon stocked, stainless steel barreled, ultra light in .338 Winchester Magnum caliber. I fired this baby in camp and you could forget about a fast second shot. The short barrel leaped up eighteen inches when fired. I've shot .375 H & H's that didn't kick nearly as bad as this weapon. To top it off, the stock was hollow, to reduce weight, and this caused a loud hollow sound every time the stock brushed up against a willow. "What do you think of 'er?" my hunter asked. "Should do the job," I lied. Now, a smart man never criticizes a man's wife, his dog or his gun.

Three days into the hunt our chance came in the form of a big grizzly feeding way up above timberline. This was not going to be an easy stalk. Our route took us across three-quarters of a mile of flat before we reached the base of the mountain. We crossed the first creek that traversed this flat with no problem. The second creek (*river*) was forty feet across, two feet deep and running swiftly over boulders. A glacier fed the stream and it was cold. We took off our hiking boots and socks and stumbled across as fast as we could. On the other side we did a gandy dance for five minutes and rubbed our lower legs to try to get some feeling back. The climb up took about two hours and then we finally eased up over a ridge to have a look at where we last saw the bear. He was there all right, ninety yards away and below, peacefully grazing on blueberries. All looked good.

I laid my hat on top of a big boulder to cushion my hunter's rifle barrel and he took aim. This bear didn't have a clue we were in the area and the shot was a complete surprise to him and me, as I couldn't believe the hunter missed by two feet. The bullet hit in front of the bear and blew chips off a rock. The bear stood up, arched his neck, dropped down and ran off out of sight. To this day, I believe the shooter simply flinched when his subconscious mind remembered the punishment this rifle dealt out.

Sometimes Murphy's Law works in your favor. Two Oregon hunters and I had been hunting in early September. Everything was working against us. The weather was hot and the early evening hunt was a bust because the moose weren't coming out until well past dark when the air was cool. The few moose we saw were all in the early morning. We almost had a bull called in at one point when the fickle breeze changed directions and gave away our scent. Another time, a cow we hadn't seen spooked and took the bull with her. The seven-day hunt was up with only one bear bagged and no moose. I said "If you boys can come back in a month I've got a five-day opening due to a late cancellation that I'll give you, free." These were fine men and hunters and I wanted their first hunt in B.C. to be a success. They jumped at the second chance and on October 15, they were back.

What a difference! We did just about everything wrong and still got moose. Bob shot his bull the second day out. The moose had winded us before we saw him and we looked up to see parts of him through the bush as he ran for the cover of the thick spruce. For some unknown reason, the moose stopped at the edge in the only open spot we could see. One shot from Bob's rifle and he buckled—one moose taken care of.

Ron's moose came the next day. It had been raining and snowing all night and morning came with no break in the weather. It looked like our old bad luck was with us again. That afternoon there was still a light drizzle mixed with snow so I decided to hunt close to home on Hoodoo Lake. We took the boat across the lake and took a short hike to a small meadow half a mile off the lake. The weather cleared up and we saw a lot of moose sign, but no moose. We headed back to the boat. We were motoring down the lake and were within sight of home when I spotted a moose standing against the timber 200 yards back off the far lakeside. I beached the boat and Ron shot. The moose ran from sight and I couldn't tell if it was a hit or not, so we hiked up to where we last saw it to look for blood. I don't know why, but I looked back across the lake and there was our moose swimming right toward the home place. We dashed the 200 yards back to the boat. We were still too far to shoot when the moose climbed up on shore and ran to the bush and freedom. Rats! Against all logic he reappeared and stepped into ankle deep water! We made no mistake this time and Ron had his winter meat supply.

# The Trapper Before Me

He had come from the old country of Lithuania. I believe he left there around 1913 as a young man. How he came to settle in the Prince George area, I don't know. His trapline trails were now my trapping trails; most of his old cabins were in ruins when I took over in 1981. He spent his life in this Salmon and Muskeg River area. It was eerie at times when I would come across his old trap sets. I would be looking for the best location to set a lynx cubby on some creek and there would be the remains of his set.

He had trapped the line in the days before snowmobiles, before any logging roads and before outboard motors, in the earliest years. A horse-drawn wagon would bring his supplies in from Chief Lake to the bank of the Salmon River near where Nukko Creek enters. This was where he kept his freight canoe. Poling, pushing, dragging and paddling he would slowly work his way up river into his trapping country to spend the winters. In his peak trapping years he used over fifteen line cabins. Cabins needed to be a day's walk apart, about seven miles. His line stretched for forty miles north to south as the crow flies. I would find his old rusty traps hanging in the trees. A man afoot can carry only so much, so the traps were never gathered up. His cabin on Muskeg Lake was still in good shape because he was forced to rebuild this one in the 1950s after a fire. A sheet of canvas hung off the door as a windbreak during the cold weather. A sheet like this had saved his life after the fire.

The wood stove had somehow caught his cabin on fire during the night. By the time he awoke, the place was in flames. Leaping out of bed with only his long johns on, he ran out the door grabbing the piece of canvas as he went. His snowshoes were hanging on the outside wall and these he saved. The temperature was well below freezing and the snow was deep. He fashioned a pair of makeshift moccasins from some of the canvas and, wrapping what remained over his shoulders, started out for his nearest cabin that had spare clothes. This was fifteen miles downstream over the frozen Muskeg River.

He was an energetic, small-framed man with a bowed back when I met him in 1972 as he chopped wood at his summer cabin on Chief Lake. Time catches up to us all. Martin Shaffer died in 1974 at eighty-six years of age. I think of him now and then as I walk his old trails.

# The Four Thousand Dollar Bullet

Sheep hunting today is a rich man's sport. In British Columbia, as in Alaska and other places, nonresidents must, by law, engage the services of a licensed big game guide and that does not come cheap. I was working as an assistant guide for an outfit that held the license to a fair sheep area west of the Klappan River. In the fall of 1981, another guide and I were taking out a couple of well-heeled sportsmen. Our quarry would be sheep and goat.

Twenty-five miles of horseback riding found us in prime game country. The shed antlers of caribou and moose indicated that this was a wintering area for the ungulates. We saw a few goats and a band of sheep, ewes and lambs on our trip in. The hunters were saddle sore but full of optimism as we hit the sack that first night. Our goat hunter filled his tag on the third day, but finding a sheep, a shootable one, wasn't going to be easy. Over the next seven days we put in some of the hardest hunting I've ever done. We saw many sheep but full-curl rams were as scarce as vestal virgins. During this time our sheep hunter, to his credit, remained lighthearted and optimistic. This hunt was costing him a bundle—$4,000 U.S. We put this office worker through the mill, up and down every day, riding and walking until all of us were beat.

On the last day of the hunt our luck changed. We had been glassing the mountain slopes from our lookout for about three hours and were about to move on when a sheep stood up 200 yards in front of us. The animal seemed to appear out of nowhere as we had looked at this spot often. He must have been bedded down out of sight and now rose to feed. The hunter had shown us his new rifle of which he was justifiably proud. It was a Ruger 30-06 with a large variable scope. The only reservation I had about his shooting iron was the fact that it was a single shot, with no chance of a quick second shot.

The sheep stood broadside in the open. The hunter had a good rest, the wind was calm. Yes, everything looked perfect. It seemed to take a long time for him to get the shot off and when he did, the rocks beneath the ram's feet exploded, a clean miss. Excitedly the hunter tried to reload his rifle, but the sheep had other ideas and was in high gear instantly. Before another shot could be taken, the sheep was gone out of sight over the crest of the hill. Our hunt was over. The hunter picked up his spent brass shell from the ground, the four thousand dollar bullet.

# Two Bears for One

"I want a big bear," my hunter said when he and his wife arrived at my home place at Hoodoo Lake. "That should be no problem," I said as we were about to start a seven-day hunt in the spring of 1993.

I wanted to start the hunt off right by sighting in his rifle at 100 yards (I should say rifles, as he brought three). He asked me to do the target shooting and I had to adjust his brand new 7 mm magnum. It shot a foot high and six inches to the left. He decided this was the rifle he would use and I assured him if he missed now it wouldn't be the rifle's fault.

The first day out we saw four black bears in four different locations. The first one was too smart for us and my hunter was not fast enough on the second bear. The last two were deemed too small. We headed home. When we got home the hunter's wife, Michelle, reported seeing a bear across the lake shortly after we left.

The next day's prospects looked good. We used my riverboat to cross the lake and have a better look at two bears feeding about 300 yards apart on the far side of the lake. The black was small but the other, a brown phase one, was a keeper if we could score. I beached the boat and we hit the bush to come out downwind from the bears. We were about half way to within shooting range and still in the bush when I saw a motion off to my right. The smaller of the two bears looked at us and bolted for the safety of the bush. We carried on to a small knoll, where we should have seen the bear in the clearing, but the big bear was nowhere to be seen.

After twenty minutes of looking around we decided to back-track toward home. We had just crossed the same knoll that we had come in on and there was our bear. Big, brown and thick haired; everything the hunter wanted was standing seventy-five feet in front of him! Now, over the fifteen years I've been guiding, I have noticed a pattern among hunters. Many are excellent shots at paper targets and good to fair shots on moose, but if there's one thing that rattles an otherwise good shot, it is a bear. My client fired and the bear turned his head to look our way; he then ran off. I could not see how my man could miss at that range, but miss he did. It was a long walk back to the boat.

We finished the day out with two more bears sighted, but neither measured up. We ate roast beef for supper, as well as "crow," thanks to my hunter's wife after she heard the story. "Not to worry. Tomorrow is a new day and you'll get another chance," I said.

The third day of the hunt, we hunted hard all morning in a new area and caught a glimpse of only one small bear. The women went to town to shop and saw six different bears. "What's the matter with you guys?" they said when they returned and met us for lunch.

That afternoon, using binoculars we glassed three or four large clearcuts that were just the right age (six to ten years after logging) for bears, but no black grazers could be found. We had given up and were headed home when a bear appeared 150 yards ahead. We closed the range to less than ninety yards. "What do you think he would go for size?" my hunter asked. Bears are tough to judge, but I guessed five and a half feet, a medium-sized bear. "That's good enough," he said, then took careful aim and fired. The bear took off into the light jack pine, but I was sure he had been hit. Both of us pussyfooted up the trail to where the bear disappeared.

I was leading, carrying my 45-70, and we reached the spot where I thought the bear had disappeared into the surrounding bush, when suddenly I heard a crack. I couldn't believe it when the bear stepped out ten feet in front of us and looked right at me. The only time I use my rifle when guiding is if an animal is wounded and in danger of getting away. I knew this one had been hit hard, so I shot him at point blank range in the chest. The bear wheeled and ran into the pines about seventy feet, collapsed and died. After a bit of whooping and back slapping, we went in the bush for the bear. We laid our rifles down to drag him out to a clearing. I started to dress the bear out and the hunter went back for the rifles.

"Hey, Bernie," he shouted, "there's another dead bear in here!" What?! Sure enough, there was a second bear down. We dragged him out alongside the first bear and the situation started to clear. Here were two identical bears, about 150 pounds each, approximately four years old, with identical facial features and color, right down to the small white patch under their chins. We had each killed a bear with one shot. We cut our tags and I gave the hunter my bear as a bonus.

The next day was spent skinning bears and boiling skulls. We hung up the four hams and backstraps in the meat shed and salted the hides. From here on in we would do some camera shooting.

After six days of hunting we had seen twenty-one different bears. There had been two sows with triplets around our place that spring and one sow with twins. I have hunted and guided for twenty-five years all over the northern half of the province and I believe the area just north of Prince George has the largest concentration of bears anywhere. There appears to be about one brown phase for every six or seven blacks. We saw one that spring that would go 300 pounds. The largest I've ever seen went approximately 450 pounds. Another hunter and I got him in 1991 and he made an honest six-foot seven-inch rug. These bears were shot in the spring and would have weighed about 100 pounds more if taken in the fall.

# The Moose We Could Not Eat

I have eaten deer when one mouthful was enough and was once in on a deer kill where the rutting smell was so bad it would knock a dog off a gut wagon. Old mountain goats can get mighty gamy although the younger ones, six years and down, are very palatable. Caribou are delicious eating, providing you get them before the mating season starts. A bull caribou never stops running while the rut is on and the lactic acid builds up to a high level in his muscles. The meat looks okay and smells fine until it is cooked; then the smell will drive you out of the cabin. Younger black bears are good eating. I like the smoked "hams" the best, but the grizzly is strictly crow bait. I've never tasted a bad moose; sure there's been the odd tough one that I probably never hung long enough to age but the meat was nevertheless tasty.

October 1977 found my brother Shawn and me waiting for a float plane on Morfee Lake just outside Mackenzie, B.C. The plane was three hours late because of morning fog that delayed departure from Prince George. We weren't bored, though, as we had been helping the Royal Canadian Mounted Police dive team look for the bodies of two boaters who drowned in the lake the previous day. Actually, there were four people on board the twelve-foot car topper when it overturned only 400 yards from shore. One man swam to shore and was recovering in hospital from exposure. The police had already found a six-year-old girl floating with her life jacket still on but, unfortunately, she had perished from the cold water. We helped the two divers unload the bodies of the man and young boy from the police boat into the waiting ambulance. We were two very sober and quiet men as we finally climbed aboard the Beaver float plane to start on our hunt.

Our destination was Tobin Lake, just north of where the Ospika River flows into Williston Lake. We were after moose meat and either a cow or bull would do to fill the freezer. After about forty-five minutes in the air, we were circling the lake with an eye for a good campsite. "Put her down near that point of land," I said to the pilot. "You mean where that moose is standing?" he asked. Sure enough, there was a moose standing looking up at the airplane. As we touched down the moose ran for parts unknown but its appearance sure was a boost for our morale.

We soon had our tent pitched, firewood laid up and even optimistically put up a game pole. What a great place this was, low mountains surrounded the lake, and the swamp at the south end sure looked "moosey." It's a great feeling to be in the wilderness with clear weather and a good hunting partner.

On the second day at the lake, we hit pay dirt. As we paddled down the lake, a moose appeared on the shore of a peninsula that jutted out into the water. As we approached, the cow ran out of sight so we just paddled around to the other side of the spit and there was our moose meat on the hoof. It took two shots from my old .270 to bring her down and I guessed her live weight would be 1,200 pounds, a big cow. As we quartered the carcass, I noticed small pea-sized white blobs surrounded by a clear halo in the meat, especially around the lower legs. I didn't say anything to Shawn but was a little worried. I'd seen these worms before in moose but not as thick as this moose had them, yet the cow looked to be in excellent shape and the liver was not spotted.

Two days after we collected my moose, Shawn got his chance. Another cow was swimming the lake and we paddled furiously to catch up to it and get within rifle range. Shawn made a clean one-shot kill as the animal beached. This moose, a young one, was very skinny and when we eviscerated the animal the intestines contained a tapeworm. I carefully pulled the worm away from the offal and, when laid out on the beach, it was over fifteen feet long! "What's with this country?" I thought, "Two moose and both had parasites."

When we arrived back home at the end of the week, I made a trip into the Ministry of Environment in Prince George to speak to the game biologist. I brought the meat from the older cow moose with me and the biologist, Mr. Child, looked it over. This was indeed a bad case of white measle worm infestation and the

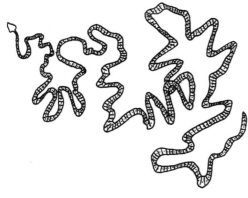

Tobin Lake area was known for the prevalence of this disease. The biologist assured me the meat would be perfectly safe for human consumption as long as it was well cooked. I said "no thanks" and asked for a new moose tag. I got the tag (for another twenty bucks). The tapeworm in the other moose was no problem as it did not infect the meat, only the intestines. The biologist claimed a moose could carry a tapeworm all its life and not suffer any serious effects. I don't think I'll hunt around the Tobin Lake country again.

# Why Guides Go Gray

I guess I've just been lucky during my years as a big game guide. For the most part I've had good sportsmen to take out. Most hunters are very particular when choosing a partner, and with good reason, considering all that could go wrong; high-powered rifles, weather and boats. Mix in wild country with emergency help at least hours away and you have lots of potential for tragedy. As a guide you are taking out complete strangers, however, so extra caution is essential.

As I said, I've been lucky with my clients but a few lemons come to mind. I like to work hard for the men so they can enjoy the whole hunting experience—the beautiful scenery and wild country. Almost all the hunters are amateur photographers and if they collect game it's a welcome bonus.

Joe (not his real name) was a killer. I could see that, for him, everything depended on the kill. He was a Disney villain in the flesh. He put every bird and small animal we saw in his sights and no doubt would have shot if I had allowed. He was not a pleasant man to be around and I wasn't sorry to see him go when his seven days were up. The best part—he never had an opportunity to shoot a thing.

Blowhard braggers are a hazard in any camp. Three of the four hunters in our camp were suffering, along with us two guides, as we listened to Mr. Big's stories. He was the foremost authority on game, rifles and calibers. He showed us his magnum rifle, a .338 Winchester Magnum he stated would knock a moose flat with one shot. "How many moose have you taken?" I asked.

"Well, none yet," he stated hesitantly, "but lots of elk."

"Moose are not elk" I told him. As most experienced hunters know, while not a hard animal to kill, moose are extremely hard to drop in their tracks. Our man had his chance the following day on the river. A big moose stood broadside ahead of us as I killed the outboard and tilted it up. We drifted within fifty yards and Mr. Big shot. I could see through the binoculars it was a good hit, right in the rib cage. The moose just stood there and took a few steps to the water's edge.

"I must have missed him," the hunter exclaimed as he chambered another round. Before I could say anything, he fired again. This time the moose was facing the opposite direction and, sure enough, I could again see it was a good shot. "Hold your fire," I shouted, "the moose is hit good and won't go far." The hunter looked at me like I was nuts as the moose walked into the riverside brush and out of sight. I beached the boat and we stepped into the woods where, sure enough, there was the dead moose not twenty yards from where we last saw him. Mr. Big was unusually quiet around the table that evening in camp.

Hunters that wander off are a worry, as the law states the guide must accompany the hunter at all times. My two hunters were seventy and fifty years old. The old-timer was easily tired, so I left him at the river trail head and took the younger man with me a mile or so to a meadow to look for game. The older gentleman assured me he would be all right and would stay put while we were gone.

Two hours later we arrived back at the river to find no sign of the hunter. We shouted and fired a round into the air—no response. Darkness was coming and I was worried. After another half-hour of looking and hollering ourselves hoarse, I heard a faint voice a long way off. We hooted back and forth in the dark, guiding the old boy in by sound. He had got turned around in the willow thickets that ran back from the river. He was scratched up, tired and scared, but otherwise okay.

One reason a guide must stay with his client is to positively identify the target as legal game. A guide I know had posted one hunter overlooking a willow flat and was taking the man's partner a few hundred yards further up the meadow to better cover the area. The two men had only just left the posted man's sight when the boom of a rifle surprised them. Rushing back, the guide asked the man what happened. He stated that a grizzly had charged him two minutes after they had left him. He said that he had to shoot it in self-defense. The guide went down the bank to the spot where the bear had disappeared into the bush. Sure enough, a little way in lay a dead grizzly; he had been shot from behind, up the rump. The reader can figure this one out for himself.

# Mountain Goat—A Tough Customer

Mountain goats don't run very often, even when shot at. They usually walk up the hill to get away as if to say "I'm not worried." Panic is not part of their character.

Four of us once saw a small herd of goats head up a slope and over the lip of the hill to the steep cliffs on the other side. They had finished feeding and, as goats like to do, they bedded down on narrow ledges with a good view of the country below. We approached the crest and peeked over to, we hoped, get some pictures. There were about fifteen goats, all nannies and kids, about twenty feet below us and completely inaccessible to a man without special mountaineering equipment. They looked up at us with apprehension but, except for one or two that stood up, the rest just sat there. We took our photos and left the herd to their rest.

Goat hunting is exciting, but only for those hunters in pretty good shape. I was guiding a couple of men from the U.S. up at the headwaters of the Skeena River. This was a general hunt and my guys had tags for bear, moose, goat and caribou. I usually like to take hunters out for moose first. This, as a rule, does not require a lot of climbing and gives the hunters a chance to get used to the hiking and me a chance to evaluate their ability.

"We want to go after goat right off the bat," Wayne and Dick said, "while we're still fresh." I didn't like the idea and pointed out where we would have to climb to get to the goats. "See that rooster comb at the top of that mountain?" I said, pointing at a 30° angle up from camp. "That's where we hunt 'em." They were not dissuaded.

We started out the next morning for the three-hour climb to the rooster comb. I noticed both men were wearing felt pack boots; the kind with leather uppers and rubber bottoms. This type of boot allows too much room and movement for the feet when climbing in steep country. The climb took seven hours up, so we ran out of hunting time fairly swiftly and had to head back to camp without seeing anything. Both hunters were limping noticeably by the time we made camp. Boots were removed to reveal four-inch wide blisters across the pads of both hunters' feet. "Let's try for moose using the boat tomorrow," Dick said.

To better your chances for goat, always try to get above them if possible. I was hunting some nice country west of the Klappan River with a professor from California. Our goat hunt was a fairly typical one—as far as goat hunting goes. We had spotted about ten goats spread out across a cliff face the day before. Now we had managed to get our horses around the back side of the cliff and up the mountain to within 200 yards of the summit. We stalked up the last bit on foot and, sure enough, there were our goats. A careful inspection of nearly twenty goats showed that at least two of the billies had good horns. We maneuvered over closer to the best one, keeping out of sight by staying on our side of the rim. The goat didn't see us as we eased our heads over the edge to look. That goat may as well have been on the moon because to shoot him where he was would have caused him to fall off a 100-foot cliff; not too good on horns and meat. We stayed out of sight and waited, hoping the goat would move away from the cliff face.

An hour passed and finally our quarry moved off to our left. When he reached a spot above a shale slope I said to the teacher, "let him have it." Boom; a miss, and at only thirty yards distance? I looked at the hunter's scope and noticed the variable adjustment was set to ten power, too high at this range. The goat didn't move as my man adjusted the scope to three power and got ready to fire again. The 30-06 bucked and his shot hit the mark; down went old billy. The shale slope was steeper than I had figured, however, and that goat flip-flopped on the loose shale for two minutes until he came to rest on some scrub balsam trees near the base of the hill. Three hours later, after going around the mountain with the horses, we approached the goat. It was a good billy with nine and five-eighth inch long horns. The small rings on the horns showed him to be six years old. My hunter was

extremely happy and the goat now stands full-mounted on a rock over his fireplace in California.

A man can get himself into trouble if he has the idea he can go wherever the goat goes. I once experienced this firsthand. My hunter had shot a good goat on the far side of a fairly steep slope that consisted of loose gravel over solid rock. The goat had crossed this slope just before we shot him and now he lay dead on the far side. The slope dropped down to a sheer drop-off 200 feet below us. I told my hunter to wait while I tested things out. The slope didn't seem too bad, even though I was sliding down a bit with each step. I worked my way halfway across to the only rock sticking up and rested there for a minute. The second half was even more slippery with the loose gravel making traction difficult. I made it across with still over fifty feet to the drop-off to spare.

I called over to my hunter and told him he had better work his way down, across and back up and not chance the slope. This would mean quite a bit more work, but it's better to be on the safe side. "Not to worry," he shouted, "if you made it, so can I." Well he managed to reach that same rock in the middle, got a bear hug on it, and froze. He wouldn't go back, couldn't go up, and was too scared to go ahead. A fine fix we were in. It took me about fifteen minutes to calm him down and talk him into crossing the rest of the way. He was pretty white-faced and shaky-legged when he finally reached me.

Mountain goats can live to be teenagers and the older the goat, the longer the horns. The real long-horned billies all have one thing in common, however, and that is good growth for their first year of life. It may be the result of an early birth, good summer or lots of mother's milk but the length of the lamb tips can mean the difference between an eight and a half inch billy and a ten-inch billy at four and a half years of age. The annual rings on the horns are a rough way to measure age but the teeth of the lower jaw give the true age. This aging is done in the laboratory and hunters in B.C. are required by law to turn in the jaw. I wonder how the lab technicians made out aging a nanny we sent in one year without a tooth left. Her horns showed about seventeen rings! She was all by herself, had a poor coat, and looked skinny. She likely would not have made another winter.

It's a sad fact but, contrary to the stories in the hunting magazines, not all sportsmen kill their animals humanely with one perfectly placed shot. No one likes to wound an animal, much less talk about it to others, but I'm telling the following story to show the tenacity to life exhibited by the mountain goat.

We spotted them from camp, about thirty goats up near the top of the mountain. I doubted there would be any decent males in this bunch of nannies and kids but my Michigan hunter was itching for a chance on a goat, so I said we would climb up for a closer look. He was used to hunting deer in his home state but this was his first trip to B.C. for mountain goat.

Two hours of climbing found us on the mountain crest about 400 yards off to one side of where we had last seen the goats. We proceeded to walk the spine of the mountain very cautiously because over each knoll could be a goat. We had traveled about 200 yards in this fashion when we saw a goat at about the same time he saw us. He was bedded down right on the trail that followed the crest. To his back was the gentle slope of the south side. In front of him, about ten feet away, was the lip of a cliff, the bottom of which I couldn't see.

The goat stood up broadside with his head turned looking at us. He arched his back and stretched; I could tell he was a good billy. "Shoot him and anchor him on the spot," I whispered to my hunter. We were no more than twenty yards from the goat. The hunter raised his rifle and fired. The goat humped up, gut shot. The second shot hit the front leg low. The goat stumbled for the safety of the cliff and fell off into space. I saw him free fall about seventy feet, hit a projecting ledge, bounce off and soar out of sight. "That goat is going to be mincemeat," I said.

We did not have much of the usual enthusiasm as we started the long climb around and down to the base of the cliff. Two hours later we were approaching the spot where I guessed the goat to be. The last part of the goat's fall was about eighty feet to a jumble of boulders. I could see him laying there about 100 feet away. You can imagine my surprise when, as I walked up to him, he lifted his head and looked right at me. I mercifully finished him off. We had an empty feeling inside as we started back to camp with this one, but I also came away with a lot more respect for the mountain goat.

# For the Record

The American sportsmen, and to a lesser extent the German hunters, show a great deal of interest in the size of the trophy. Will it make the record book? The Canadian hunter is more interested in filling the freezer. Oh, most of the Americans I've guided want the meat all right, but I hear a lot of talk about the Boone & Crockett, Safari Club or Pope & Young record books of the largest game heads taken. This can get a little out of hand at times and I tell my hunters that some of the greatest trophies are not even recorded in the book so these "world's records" must be taken with a grain of salt. Witness the following story.

I worked alongside Bill Love, Sr. for a few years and can attest to his integrity and experience. At one time, Bill's outfit had produced seven out of the top ten grizzlies taken with a bow as recorded in the Pope & Young record book. Bill knew his bears and had personally been the guide for most of these bears. In the early 1980s, Bill was taking out an American client to hunt grizzly using a bow and arrow.

It was early September and the weather was holding fair. A hunter had taken a good caribou above timberline a week before Bill and his client came into the area to hunt bear. On the second day of their hunt a bear was spotted from camp feeding on the remains of the caribou. The spotting scope got the men's hearts racing when they saw the gigantic size of the animal. They took note of the bear's path when he went to and from the kill. The following morning was spent climbing the mountain to lay an ambush for the bear on his usual route. The two men had been in position behind a boulder for about two hours when the bear, a creature of habit, followed his trail of yesterday. Now, a grizzly bear can only be taken safely with a bow when he is positioned correctly for the hunter. A perfect position is with the animal quartering slightly away from the hunter and no more than thirty yards distant.

The excited men waited behind their rock and, by peeking around its side, could see the bear's approach. They waited until the bear passed them and then they eased out for the shot. The bear was looking down the trail when the arrow hit him just behind the ribs, penetrating to the fletching. He leapt ahead and ran out of sight over the lip of a small hill. Bill cautiously approached with his backup rifle in his hands. They could hear the bear roaring and then sudden silence. A finishing shot was not necessary.

The bear died without falling over on his side but just crouched down like a dog with his chin resting on the ground. This was a bear! His grizzled hump was over waist high on the men as they stood beside it. Of course there was no way to accurately weigh the animal, but I believe Bill's educated guess of 1,200 pounds. That's a terrific size for a mountain grizzly that normally averages 500 to 600 pounds for a full-grown male. His head was large as well and this is important for the record book. Measured green, the skull scored over thirty inches. (This represents the total of length plus width.)

After skinning the bear, the men took a few measurements with Bill's steel tape. The width around the chest at the armpits was ninety-eight inches and the width around the neck was forty-eight inches. I've forgotten the length of the hide but it was huge. This bear would be a new world record but such was not to be. You see, the hunter was a practicing veterinary doctor in his home state of California. He came from an area that had more than its share of radical animal rights groups and the publicity that would follow a new world record might not be so good for his business. To this day, the North American record grizzly bear is not even listed in the books.

Real trophies must be judged using more than a measuring tape. I was guiding a fine gentleman and sportsman from Oregon at the headwaters of the Finlay River one fall. This would probably be Jim's first and last hunt in the mountains he loved. You see, Jim was going blind at forty years of age. He had enjoyed hunting his native state for deer and elk for many years and, for a gift, his wife saved her money to send Jim on this B.C. hunt before it was too late.

On our first day out, I took Jim and another hunter up a swampy meadow looking for moose. A bull caribou came out of nowhere and ran up to us out of curiosity. Jim was directly behind me and I motioned him to step ahead and shoot as this was a good bull. He instead whispered to the other man to take the first chance which he did, and he missed.

Jim's chance came again a few days later as we motored up the lake. I could see through my binoculars some kind of animal walking the shore on the far side a mile from us. As we neared, I told Jim it was a caribou, but just a mediocre one. He took a good look and said that it would be just fine. I shut the boat motor off and, at 100 yards, the 30-06 boomed. The caribou dropped instantly, a clean kill. Back at camp that afternoon I carefully skinned out the head for a full shoulder head mount. Jim was extremely pleased and couldn't thank me enough for helping him get his last trophy. That caribou now hangs on the wall in Jim's home in Portland, a trophy from a hunt he'll always remember.

# In the Past

When the first white men arrived in northern British Columbia they were agents of the big fur trading companies (The Hudson's Bay Company or The North West Company). It was these men, Scottish, French and English, that taught the Natives how to trap the fur bearers. The Indians, to their credit, did manage to catch small mammals using the dead fall trap or snares, but most of their small game was for personal use. They were adept at hunting big game as their lives depended on wild meat, especially the tribes not located on the salmon streams. It was the white man, however, who supplied the steel traps and the know how to the Indians and they could not have taught better people. Soon the trading posts throughout the north were being supplied with the finest wild furs, almost all being trapped by the Natives.

I have had the opportunity to hunt and trap with both Carrier and Cree Indians. In the fall of 1977, I was drifting a small river sixty miles north of Prince George with a Cree Indian from the Rocky Mountain foothills area. We had been on the river for two days. On the morning of the third day, we got into some action. The river was snaking back and forth and as we approached a sharp bend we could hear splashing from around the corner. Ted looked back at me from the bow and I nodded. Keeping my paddle in the water, I used a variation of the J-stroke to move the canoe in perfect silence around the bend. Thirty yards in front of us were two cow moose and a bull. Ted raised his 30-30 and fired at the bull. He shot it Indian style, that is, dead center of the hump. This shot, if done right, results in the animal dropping as if pole axed. So it was with this moose.

Ted explained that the Indians around the Grande Prairie area often did not have rifles even as large as the modest 30-30 Winchester caliber. They found the hump shot worked best. He also described how in the past the Indians used many parts of moose that the average hunters of today, Indian and white, do not use. The stomach, the washed out small intestine, the tendons and sinew, the hide and the moose's bell (used for a "possibles" pouch), and even the moose's nose, were either made into something or eaten. A man could tell by what was left behind whether the moose had been killed by a white man or Indian. It used to be said the Indian ate everything but the grunt.

The best man I've ever known on the river was a Carrier Indian guide and outfitter named Art Bracey. Art showed me many tricks when I guided and trapped with him. He taught me how to pole a boat, which is still the best way to maneuver a canoe up stream. I learned from him how easy it is to steer a row boat when going downstream by sitting up in the bow and drifting backwards. I still have an excellent beaver skinning knife Art made for me when we traveled together spring beaver trapping. The knife is handmade out of a hacksaw blade. Indians in the old days could not always afford factory-made items and made do with whatever was handy.

Alas, as much as it is now in vogue for the Indians to talk about their heritage and wanting to go back to the land, the fact is that the vast majority of Natives like the comfort and modern conveniences of the cities and towns, just as non-Natives do. The harsh life on the trapline is not for them. In fact, the majority of the wild fur sold annually from B.C. is now caught by non-Natives. Each summer I travel to Fort St. James to visit Lazzar and Betsy Pious, Carrier Indians, to lease their trapline for another year. Their line complements my own registered trapline and gives me more area to work. I have leased this line from them and the late Jim Sagalon for over ten years. On one of my trips to the Fort, on a hot July day, I sat with about ten local Natives on the bank of Stuart Lake and had three different men wanting to lease me their lines.

I once gave a ride to a Fort St. James elder by the name of Johnny Sam. Johnny was also a Carrier Indian who trapped the Great Beaver Lake area. Johnny's snowmobile broke down and he had walked out to a forest road where I picked him up. I could see he was all in, as he was in his late sixties. We had a good visit as we traveled the fifty miles into town. During the conversation he lamented the fact that none of his children were interested in taking over the trapping business and his generation might be the last to carry on the old ways.

An admirable trait of the Indians is their respect for the game they hunt. I try to instill this respect in my hunters. When a large mammal such as the moose is taken, I don't like to immediately start cutting it up. I like to sit back and admire the animal for the gift that it is to us. The wild country of northern B.C. would be nothing but nice scenery without the wildlife that abounds in it. The wild animals supply my livelihood and my reason for being here.

# Mistakes Can Kill

The place, Summit Lake just north of Prince George; the scene, two men in a canoe paddling quietly across the lake on a misty fall morning looking for moose. A shot was fired followed by several more. One man in the canoe was killed and the other wounded. A tragic accident, for sure. How could a hunter on shore mistake these men for a moose? He stated to the police afterwards that he thought it was a moose swimming the lake. One canoeist was even wearing blaze orange!

My good friend Staff Sergeant Leland McLean (of the RCMP) was involved in the investigation of this early 1970s case. The RCMP, with McLean, reenacted the incident several days later when conditions were identical. There was a slight early morning mist rising from the lake and the man posted on shore was standing in the exact spot where the shots were fired from. The two officers were dressed the same as the victims and were paddling the canoe over the same place on the lake. Staff Sergeant McLean was the man on shore and he told me afterwards that the two men in the canoe looked exactly like two men in a canoe. I'll let the reader judge this one.

Hunting is a safe sport but accidents occasionally occur. I've seen hunters driving pickups slowly along the bush roads when they were too drunk for their own safety or anyone else's. Hunting and booze don't mix. Around 1988 a good example of this occurred.

I was beaver trapping on the river in early May and had just arrived at my small cabin at the junction of the Muskeg and Salmon Rivers. I fired up my wood heater and went down to the river to get a pail of water. There's a bad log jam across the river there, one of several on the Salmon that block off the river from shore to shore. The spring runoff was at its height and deep brown water was surging and boiling around and through the jam. I spotted a canoe bow pointing up from the logs. As I climbed over the logs to get a better look, I noticed a life jacket, paddle and thermos floating around in circles in a back eddy. I could see that the canoe, with outboard still attached, was bent in half. I found no sign of survivors and nothing in my cabin had been used.

I drove out the thirty miles to home and notified the police. The next day I guided the RCMP to the spot. With their winch and truck, they pulled out the canoe and retrieved all the floating gear. The thermos was nearly empty, with about an inch of liquid left. The liquid smelled like whiskey.

The following day I again accompanied the constable and we looked downstream for three miles, up to the next log jam that blocked the river. We expected to see this jam comb out any bodies, but found nothing. The police notified the local newspaper and they ran a story "Canoe Mystery" the next day. This brought results. A man in his late thirties showed up to claim the boat and gear. It seems this sport was spring bear hunting, and celebrating as well, when he decided to canoe over the jam instead of portaging around it. He stated that he was so embarrassed about the incident that he didn't want his buddies to find out about it. He walked all night for fourteen hours to Nukko Lake Store to get to a phone. To this day there is an expensive .300 Weatherby Magnum somewhere under the logs on the Salmon River.

Not all hunting accidents end so well. A good friend of mine, also a guide, experienced a tragic accident in the mountains north of Smithers, B.C. one fall. He and another younger assistant guide were taking out two U.S. hunters, who had been hunting partners and best of friends for years. The two guides decided to take one hunter each and each duo would walk along the side of a ravine that had a good willow-banked stream running along the bottom. They were hunting for moose. Occasionally the men could see one another across the ravine. They worked their way along in this fashion for some time and hadn't seen each other because of thick bush for fifteen or twenty minutes. When both parties again were across from one another about 100 yards separated them.

At first sight of the other pair, the hunter accompanied by the young guide whispered "moose" to the guide and instantly raised up his rifle. The guide recognized the men at once but was only able to say "Hold it! It's the guys"—boom—too late. The 30-06 bullet traveled across the canyon and drove through the neck of his friend, the other hunter. The other guide was beside the victim, but slightly higher up because of the steep sided hill. The same bullet caught him in the thigh muscle and went right through. The hunter died instantly and the guide was several months in hospital while his leg healed.

The other hunter? He sold his rifles and has never hunted again.

Most hunting accidents are not accidents at all. Usually these incidents are because of human carelessness, buck fever, drink or inexperience. A true accident is just that, an accident; no one could have reasonably prevented it from happening. This is very rare, but I had a hunter relate to me a story of an accident that occurred in Saskatchewan several years ago.

Three hunting buddies were looking for deer in the flat pop-lar country of northern Saskatchewan. The weather had been cold for about a week, -20° to -30° every night. This particular morn-ing one fellow decided to stay in camp. The other two split up about 100 yards apart and walked parallel to one another, trying to drive out a deer.

They proceeded in this fashion for about fifteen minutes when one hunter spotted a deer thirty yards ahead. He could just see the deer's head and neck through the poplars. He fired and ejected the empty casing, but before he could get off a second shot, the buck ran off. Indeed it was a miss, for when the hunter moved up he found where the bullet had grazed a tree near where the deer had stood. The hunter then retraced his steps back to camp as it was getting late.

"No sign of Joe yet?" he asked his pal back at camp. No, Joe had not arrived, and darkness found both men worrying about their partner. In the morning both men started a search. It was not hard to pick up the trail in the snow and it led them to a grisly sight. There was Joe dead and cold.

The one hunter looked suspiciously at his buddy when he remembered the one shot he had heard while he was in camp the previous evening. The Royal Canadian Mounted Police were called in. They, too, were very suspicious of the hunter who had gone out the evening before with the victim. The man protested his innocence. The police decided to go over the events of the night before, step by step. They found the spot where the hunter had stood when he shot. They found the spent cartridge. They were even shown where the bullet had hit the tree.

The RCMP deserve a lot of credit for the rest of the story falling into place. The police traced the bullet path from the first tree where it careened off at a 90° angle, to a second tree. It had ricocheted off the second tree to a third frozen tree some distance away where it yet again bounced off. The mostly spent bullet (by then completing a U-turn) traveled a further fifty yards and hit the unfortunate hunter in the neck, killing him instantly. The man was still over 100 yards from the shooter when he met his maker. Now that was an accident!

# Anecdotes on Moose

### Antler Display

When a moose reaches full maturity he has a peak time in his life that ranges from five to ten years of age. By peak, I mean he is a veteran of many battles and is very confident in himself. I have watched big bulls square off against each other on numerous occasions and have noticed that often they will display their antlers to one another. The bull cocks his head slightly to the side and, holding his head high, will slowly move the antlers up and down or from side to side. I've seen big bulls do this to hunters just before they run off, as if they are taunting you and kind of saying, "See this, I'm not really scared of you."

### Divers

A moose, as we all know, is very much at home in the water but not every hunter has seen how good a diver a moose is. I once watched a cow moose diving in a lake that, when I checked later, was about twenty-five feet deep. The cow would completely submerge for about three minutes at a time and then reappear with a mouthful of bottom weeds. After watching her go down for a bite, a fisherman and I quietly paddled our canoe up to a spot where we figured she would surface. Sure enough, we were no more than fifteen feet from her when she surfaced and my client got a terrific picture of one astonished moose.

### Traveling Bulls

During the rut the bulls, especially the mature ones, will travel great distances to find a cow in heat. We once followed the tracks of a bull that was no more than an hour ahead of us. A blind man could have followed the animal in the four inches of fresh snow that had just finished falling. We stayed on the trail for about three miles, then gave up. I told the men that this was a traveling bull and unless we had a cow tied up ahead he was never going to stop; in fact, not once in that three miles did we see any sign of him letting up his steady long stride.

I once had two Los Angeles policemen three-quarters of the way up a mountain that we were climbing for mountain goat. We stopped to glass the river valley spread out below us. Far down in the valley, I would say about three miles away, one hunter spotted a big moose. We watched the moose for about fifteen minutes and he was keeping a steady pace, a pace too fast for a man to keep up with. I had a young assistant guide with me and I told him to take one hunter and intercept the moose below us. Brian took the American down as fast as he could and they had just bottomed out on the river flat when the moose came into sight. It took three shots from the hunter's .300 Winchester Magnum to bring the big guy down. The moose had traveled five miles from where we first glimpsed him.

## Blind Rut

The moose breeding season runs for about three weeks in our part of the country, usually from September 20 to October 15, but right in the middle of this rut, as it is called, is a peak time when some bulls go into what I call a blind rut. We've all seen hockey players that get into a fight with another player and sometimes get so worked up that they take on the entire opposing team's bench and maybe even the referee. These men have gone berserk and have to be restrained by their teammates. A moose does the same thing. I've seen bull moose so worked up that they have absolutely no caution left around hunters. At this time they can be very dangerous; gunfire, shouts, a man's scent—nothing fazes them.

I have heard fighting bulls grunting and squealing all night long. I once walked into a grove of big cottonwood trees one morning to retrieve a moose I had shot, a bull that had been fighting all night with another. The second bull left with a cow as I approached. The ground was all torn up, most of the willows were flattened; it looked like someone with a tractor and discs had gone to work. The bull I'd shot had broken off the large palmated part of one side with only the brow tine left. It must have been quite a battle.

## Female Scent

I once remarked to my old uncle Felix, a man with eighty years under his belt, that I was following a moose track in a skiff of snow one late fall day and noticed brown spots in the snow every so often. It looked like someone had gone along with an eyedropper of iodine. Felix had spent the depression in northern Manitoba trapping for a living and had learned a thing or two. He said the spots were a discharge from a cow moose in estrous and she wouldn't go far before a bull would pick up the smell she was excreting. My uncle told me when he found these spots it was just a short time before he had his bull hanging from the cabin rafters.

## Late Rut

The rut is usually over by the time I start my land trapping in

November. Many wildlife biologists are not aware of the second rut that takes place in early December. Almost every year will see a cow or cows running with a bull in December. These are cows that have not "caught" during the early rut and cycle again in early winter. The product of this late romance is not born in the usual period (late May), but instead the calf is born in August, the gestation period being about eight months. This calf goes into the following winter somewhat runty and will have a hard time if the winter snows are deep. These calves are very easy pickings for the wolves, as well.

I once shot what I believed was a calf moose during the "calf only" season. As I walked up to the dead moose I realized this animal was too big to be a calf. I was in trouble, as only two-point or smaller bulls, or calves were open season. This animal had no antlers—or did it? As I looked closer I discovered to my relief that it was indeed a yearling bull, although a very small one. It carried a bony plate on one side of its head and a four-inch long tine on the other side. This undoubtedly was a moose conceived during the late rut and born fourteen months earlier.

## Fear of Wolves

I had a chance to see the panic wolves instill in some moose. I was guiding a fisherman on the Firesteel River in northern B.C. one fine July day. The mountain scenery was magnificent, the rainbow trout were biting and we were enjoying the sight of a young bull moose feeding on shore 200 yards away. My client wanted some close-up photos of the moose so I rowed the boat in closer. The moose stood for a few camera clicks at thirty yards and then ran off, crashing through the bush as it went.

About twenty minutes later, we again heard crashing sounds and our moose was back; this time he had his hackles up, was frothing at the mouth and was breathing heavily. The moose saw us but paid us no mind and, standing in three feet of water, looked back in the direction he had just come. Then we heard them. A pack of wolves set up to howling 200 yards up the hill from the lake. They may have seen us, as they never continued the chase, but vented their displeasure by howling. The moose then swam past us to the other side of the river—to safety.

# Lost in the Bush

The horror stories of what lost men have done to compound their dilemma are hard to believe. In a blind panic, victims have been known to throw off most of their warm clothes, drop their rifles and packs and even run out of their boots in muddy country. Until a man has been lost, he doesn't exactly know just what he would do, but training and preparation beforehand can make a big difference. Fortunately,  very few people will react in the above extreme.

It's been my experience that the so-called natural sense of direction is a myth. A good sense of direction comes with experience and, above all, paying close attention to your surroundings. Take, for example, a simple thing like leaving by boat from shore. It's surprising how many people never look back at the shore to make a mental note of what the launch site looked like as they leave the beach. When they return, they have to travel up and down the shoreline looking for their trailhead. The same holds true when leaving the timber to enter a large moose meadow. There's nothing worse than coming back in semidarkness with a moose quarter strapped to your back and having to waste time and energy wandering around a soggy swamp because you can't find the trail. I've learned this lesson the hard way on a few occasions.

Traveling in the mountains I always find it relatively easy to find my way, as the landmarks are excellent. In the flat bushland of the central interior of the province, it is a different story. When the bush is so thick that even the mosquitoes have to fly single file, I always keep my map and compass handy. One without the other is of limited value. If I see a lake is northwest of where I'm standing as I look at my map, I know it is southeast when I want to return. Often I'll use the compass to start on my journey and note where the sun is. If the distance I'm traveling is relatively short, I can then put my compass in my pocket and use the sun to keep me in a straight line. If a man knows where he is in relation to his map and trusts his compass he will never truly be lost; oh, he might get turned around now and again, or it may take him longer to get out to a road than he reckoned on, but he will always find his way...eventually.

I was embarrassed. We had just made a complete circle and were right back where we started from—some guide I was. I knew this country like the back of my hand. I was taking my two hunters up a willow-choked flat into a lake. We had left a grass covered meadow for the lake and I didn't bother with my compass, instead trusting my natural sense of direction. That was all I was using, too, as the leaden sky did not even let the sun cast a shadow. We traveled for fifteen minutes and I couldn't figure out why we had not reached our destination yet. I had been pointing out moose tracks to the men and must have had my head down a lot, when finally we came to a moose meadow I didn't know existed. I dug out my topographical map and could not find this

meadow on it. We stepped out into the meadow and things began to look familiar. "Hey, there's that rub tree we were looking at this morning" one of my hunters exclaimed. Sure enough, we were right back at our grassy meadow.

I remember once when I was working for Wilderness Outfitters and had a couple of hunters with me who became thoroughly confused. My boss and owner of the outfit, Randy Wilson, had packed us in with the horses to a remote lake sixty miles north of Prince George. We had no luck after hunting Louise Lake for three days, so I decided to leave one morning for a small unnamed lake about two miles away. This lake was perhaps only 300 yards in diameter. There was no trail; no landmarks, not even a creek bed to follow. I just took a careful bearing with my compass and map, noted the sun was over my right shoulder and made a beeline for the lake. The hunters had not seen me take out the compass and I didn't use it again. We arrived dead center of the lake forty-five minutes later. The country was flat and covered with monotonous poplar trees around the lake.

On the way out, everything looked the same except now there was no sun because of overcast. Part way out we stopped for a break and when it was time to continue, I asked my hunters which way to go. Both were sure it was where they pointed; the trouble was they both pointed in opposite directions and both the wrong way. I showed them my guide's natural sense of direction; I was holding it in my hand, my compass. I showed them the bearing I took on the way in and the 180° opposite bearing we required to find our way out. They were both believers in the compass as we rounded the bend to see the cabin up ahead.

My horse, Judge, had been in this remote country often. I was guiding for Skeena Mountain Outfitters, thirty miles east of Kiniskan Lake in northwest B.C. and this was my first trip to this great country. I had spent the better part of the day getting my hunter into shooting range of a big billy goat and he made no mistake when it came down to the shooting. The trouble was, it was getting dark by the time we finished skinning and packing up the goat. We were a long way from camp, about seven miles. In those miles we had taken a torturous route to get to the goat. We had followed various creeks and draws, gone over hills and around mountains. I had been paying very close attention to the lay of the land as we came in, but I didn't have a hope of finding my way back in the dark, so I figured to bivouac at the nearest creek for the night. As we rode in total darkness, I noticed old Judge seemed to know where he was going. A few times I wanted to go right and he would always arc back to the left. "Okay, Judge, fly at it," I said to myself.

Two hours later I could see the flicker of our campfire and the silhouette of the other two men in camp. Old Judge had taken us right into camp like it was nothing. I said nothing to my hunter and, as the other guide and I were rubbing down the horses, I overheard him talking to the other hunter at the cmpfire. "That Bernie is quite a guide; he got us back to camp in pitch darkness!"

# The Weapon

A Canadian veteran of World War II once told me how he was wounded in the Italian campaign. He had been shot in the shoulder blade with a high powered sniper's rifle not unlike the big game rifle used by today's sportsman. "It felt like someone had slapped me hard on my back with no shirt on," he recalled, "and then I lost the feeling as my upper back and shoulder went numb." He went on to say that the adrenalin rush from the battle and subsequent shock afterwards prevented him from feeling much pain; that came thirty minutes later as he was being evacuated by a rough-riding jeep to hospital. I think it's safe to say the effect on a wild animal would be the same. If the bullet strikes the animal's vital organs death comes before any significant pain. This is without a doubt the quickest and most painless death that can ever befall any wild animal in nature. I can respect the nonhunter's distaste for the hunting of big game, but not on grounds of cruelty for he must consider nature's methods.

There are no old folks' rest homes for the fauna in nature. Only man has the luxury of dying of old age in a bed. Two grim realities usually face all wild creatures, death by starvation or death under the fang. When an animal is past its prime, it becomes increasingly more difficult to find food, especially for the carnivores, and slow death by starvation occurs. The ungulates' death is usually preceded by the loss of teeth, making it impossible for them to chew their food properly. A solitary mountain goat I once observed is a case in point. This female was down to skin and bones in September when she should have been fat from the past summer's grass. Females are nearly always found with the herd, but this one could no longer keep up, she would never see spring.

One January, we observed a calf moose near our home. For unknown reasons the calf was an orphan. The snow that winter

(1984) was deep, about four and a half feet on the flat. A cow moose usually breaks trail for her offspring when the drifts are deep. This young moose had no mother to do this job and had exhausted itself. It now gave up the snow-covered willow flats around Hoodoo Lake for the easy going on the plowed road. The trouble was the high snow banks covered what little feed could be found there. A week later we again saw the moose and it had died of starvation. My neighbor, Dennis Kemp, and I examined the animal and we could count its ribs.

I've already put pen to the second reality earlier in this book. Suffice to say death at the jaws of the major predators is not a pretty sight and, in the majority of cases, is not quick or painless. With all of the above in mind, two important responsibilities befall the sportsman. He must always try to place his bullets into the vital area of his target, even if it means passing up risky shots, and always use a weapon with sufficient killing ability for the game being pursued. It seems any book on hunting worth its salt devotes a chapter to rifles and calibers.

I'm definitely not an expert when it comes to the myriad of guns and bullets on the market today, but I believe I have some valid observations to offer the sportsman from the years I've guided as well as my own hunting success. A big game guide is in a unique position compared with the average sportsman. There is a limit of one big game tag for each species of animal per annum, hence the average hunter will witness only the shooting of one or two animals each year. A guide will see perhaps twenty successful hunts per season. He is watching the action calmly from the hunters side and usually keeps his binoculars trained on the animal to see if the bullet connected. The shooter himself will automatically blink at the shot and this, coupled with the rifle's recoil, usually will take his eye off the target at the critical moment of impact. The guide must be at the ready to dispatch the animal quickly if it is only wounded, and this happens frequently, especially with bears. I've seen the results of the various calibers firsthand over many years and have drawn some conclusions.

The so-called "knock down power" of a bullet is completely overrated and misunderstood by many hunters I've had in camp.

139

When the various magnum calibers come out of the gun case, often I hear stories of how this or that deer or elk was flattened by the bullet, literally knocked off its feet. I even had one hunter tell me he pushed back a grizzly three feet when he hit the bear in the chest with his .375 H & H Magnum. I say baloney.

Even the mighty .375 H & H Magnum with a 300-grain bullet, an elephant gun, (and I've seen moose hunters armed with these cannons) will not knock a 100-pound anvil off a block of wood. The same anvil that I can easily kick off with my leg. The laws of physics apply even to favorite rifles, for every action there is an opposite and equal reaction. If the fired bullet could possibly knock a 250-pound mule deer off its feet, it would knock the 200-pound hunter on his derriere when he shot it out the gun.

I stated elsewhere in this book that our largest animal, the moose, is not a hard animal to kill but is very hard to drop in his tracks. The moose is a big animal and even shot through the lungs will often wander off thirty yards or so before the bullet's effect puts him down on the ground. He's dead on his feet but just doesn't know it yet. The 30-06 class of rifle is more than adequate for this, the largest deer. The .303 British, Canada's old army service rifle, has taken more moose than any other caliber including the 30-30. The 30-30 itself is adequate for moose (I've seen several shot with this caliber) if, and I stress if, what the hunter lacks in fire power is made up for with skill and knowledge, no long shots attempted and good bullet placement.

A big bull moose shot in the ribs at close range with a 30-30, is a dead animal. The last ten years I've noticed many hunters choosing the .338 Winchester Magnum for their moose medicine and, fired from a reasonably heavy rifle, it works well. The problem with a lot of the magnums now is the trend to lighter and lighter rifles. The ultra-lights may be okay for the .270 but not for the big magnums; they just plain and simple kick too much for most men to use without flinching. I had a hunter this past fall attempting to shoot a nice-antlered bull moose. He had forgotten to take the safety off and, when he pulled the trigger, he must have jerked that rifle muzzle up twelve inches. I told him to take the safety off and to slowly squeeze the trigger on the next attempt. He missed his second shot also.

The grizzly can be a dangerous animal and that is an under-statement. My experience with grizzlies is limited, but I would say it is a lot more than most hunters have experienced. When choosing a caliber for this bear, keep two things in mind; its size and its capacity to kill you if things go wrong. My experience has been with the mountain grizzly of interior British Columbia and the average boar will go 500 pounds live weight, the females 350 pounds. This may come as a surprise to some as it seems in most tales of this animal they are all 1,000 pounds or more. These bears may come from a different part of the mountains than I come from.

I've been in on a few kills and watched many grizzly bears for hours. I once saw a huge silver tip feeding near the Edozadelli Plateau and tried to maneuver my two hunters within shooting range. The tricky mountain breeze ruined our stalk. I can still picture the bear as it ran across the mountain to get away, his beautiful coat rippling as he went. I would say this bear was 750 pounds. I almost bumped into a bush grizzly near Prince George one fall and they are usually heavier than the mountain variety. He looked, at thirty feet from me, to be around 600 pounds. The largest grizzly (taken from the Parsnip River area) I've ever seen was full-mounted by the hunter and I'm sure would go 900 pounds. This was a big ugly bush grizzly that nearly killed the guide. The point I'm making is that I've never seen a grizzly that was bigger than a full-grown bull moose, so again a 30-06 class of rifle is plenty of fire power in most cases. There is one exception, a very important exception, and that is when a grizzly is only wounded.

I once made a nice stalk on a typical mountain grizzly and killed the unsuspecting animal with one 150-grain bullet from my .270. The bear rolled down the mountain toward me after the shot and was dead almost at my feet. This bear, if only wounded, could have charged as wounded grizzlies are want to do and I could have been undergunned. As with all game, that all-important shot placement is paramount.

I've never seen a grizzly as thick through the chest as a big bull moose. The moose has very hard ribs protecting its heart lung area; by comparison all bears have fairly soft ribs. I've taken over twenty-five moose with my .270 and most of the bullets usually go right through the animal or are found just under the hide after passing through the animal. There is no reason this rifle cannot be used on the grizzly, but let's go back to the exception.

A charging grizzly is bad news. The animal can go a terrific distance when his blood is up. Stories are legend of the big bears traveling up to 100 yards with a shot-out heart and then mauling the author of the hurt. This ability was explained by a doctor once. It seems the amount of blood already in the head of the bear is enough to sustain its brain for these murderous charges without any new supply being pumped in. The bears' ability to hibernate with the corresponding slow heart rate no doubt comes into play, he simply can get by without his heart for a surprisingly long time. This is precisely the reason I like to carry my 45-70 caliber Marlin when I'm guiding clients for bear. I handload 500 grain bullets to the maximum safe limit. This big bullet can be depended upon to buck the brush and still bust a bear's skull if need be. The big magnums, as well as the twelve-gauge shotgun loaded with slugs, would all be welcome when a bear comes with homicidal intent. I'll close this diatribe on rifles with an interesting true story.

My old hunting pal and fellow guide Bill Love Sr. (now retired) was guiding none other than "Mr. Bow and Arrow" himself, Fred Bear, back in the 1960s. They were hunting the big grizzly of the upper Kispiox Valley. These bears are a bit bigger than the average mountain grizzly as they have access to the salmon spawning streams. Fred was using an ordinary recurve bow as this was before the days of the compound. Bill was walking ahead of Fred and Fred's hunting partner who was also a bow hunter. Bill had his head down, looking at the tracks of a large bear printed in the sand along the shore of the Kispiox. The running water prevented Bill from hearing a grizzly charge across the shallow stream and come right at the three men. The two hunters only had time to say "Watch it, Bill, here he comes!" Bill looked up to see the bear closing in fast. In one motion, he raised his backup rifle, a .270, and fired at the bear's head. The bear collapsed ten feet from the men and skidded to a stop on its belly. Bill had brained the bruin and killed it instantly with one 150-grain bullet. Fred and the other hunter were badly shaken by the event and when Fred came back the following year he presented Bill with a gift, a brand new Winchester in .375 H & H Magnum caliber. "There," Fred said, "I want to see you around for a few more years, Bill."

# In Hunting Shape

The physical condition of a man endeavoring to venture after mountain game is not to be taken lightly. Most men I've guided have been reasonably successful in their business life and can afford the considerable cost of a guided big game hunt. Unfortunately, the good life that comes with wealth leaves many with a few extra pounds of table muscle. I remember a big man one past hunting season, an ex-football player, who told me, "I once had the body of a Greek god but now I look like a gol' darn Greek." Joe was more than a little overweight and puffed like a locomotive on steep ground. It didn't seem to dampen his enthusiasm, however, and he managed to get around well enough to take two bears and a moose.

On another hunt, my hunter named Wes was about fifty-five years old and looked every day of it. He was on his first hunt for mountain goat and I was his guide for the ten-day trip. His hunting partner Dirk was younger and considerably thinner. Our first few days of hunting were eventful. Dirk got a good black bear one frosty morning only two hours from camp and we also spotted several moose. This had been flat-land hunting and served to get the men's city legs in shape for the assault on the lofty crags where the goats were found.

We left camp early and crossed the small lake by boat. Our route lay alongside a small feeder stream running into another lake and then the trail began to wind its way up the foothill to the mountain we would climb. Once we reached the base of the mountain, the work began in earnest and I noticed Wes was having to rest a lot to catch his breath. This was fine with Dirk and me. We weren't out to race each other to the top and the last thing I wanted to do was ruin a man's hunt and his pride by breaking him down on his vacation. The climb to the top usually took about two hours, but it took us about twice that long. I showed Wes how to take small steps and to go back and forth on the steepest slopes, but by the time we crested out on top he was all in. I called for a stop and made a pot of coffee from a small stream of snow-melt water. The cliffs about us were enshrouded in clouds but as we drank the last of the coffee the clouds dispersed to reveal a great big billy goat climbing slowly up the rock face. The goat had seen us and kept moving until the clouds again moved in.

We waited for about two hours but never saw the goat again. Wes was getting tired again from climbing around the rocks so I decided it would be best to begin our descent. Now, climbing up is hardest on the lungs, but going down is hardest on the legs, especially the knees and Wes' knees were giving him trouble. I cut him a walking stick like the European mountaineers use and that seemed to help. We had come about a third of the way down the mountain when Wes began to have real trouble. He was beginning to stagger from side to side and fell once, his rifle hitting the rocks hard. I took his small backpack, Dirk carried his rifle and we pressed on. We just made the timber of the foothills when Wes stopped, almost fell over and then sat down at the base of a tree. "You don't have a chocolate bar in your pack, do you Dirk?" he asked. Wes now disclosed the fact that he was a diabetic and had let his blood sugar go down too low. I didn't have any sugar left and neither did Dirk. We still had more than two miles to go to the boat and darkness would soon be here. My mother always wanted me to be a priest.

Wes discovered some chewing gum in his pocket and, with it and luck, we finally got to the boat using my flashlight. Back at the cabin with a good meal in him and a good night's rest, Wes was soon his old good-natured self. We never did get that goat, but Wes got a nice bull moose later in the hunt.

# Some Come Hard

Moose are denizens of the marshy lake shore and lowland muskeg country—that's what the encyclopedia tells us. Some hunters
are unaware that this large deer is very often found and hunted
well above tree line in the mountainous country of British Columbia. The drawback here is that the sportsman has a tough
climb to reach these animals and a big job packing the meat down
if he connects.

"What are you looking up there for?" my hunter asked, and I
knew he thought I should be looking, instead of up, down along
the river valley. I mentioned to Mike and Dave, my clients, that
sometimes during the breeding season the bull moose will drive
his cow or cows up to the high country. He does this to keep his
girl friends away from other suitors and the cows don't seem to
mind. In fact, there are certain plants that the moose will graze
on that only grow above timberline and to get at these morsels
I've seen them kneel down to eat, as their legs are too long
normally to graze standing up. There is also the added bonus of
no insects up high where the frosts come early.

We'd spent an hour or so looking through our binoculars
when Mike shouted, "Moose!" Sure enough, 1,500 feet above us
and across the valley was the bull moose and two cows. They
seemed to appear out of nowhere, but must have been hidden in
a draw. We started our long stalk.

It took us about an hour to clear the last of the scrub balsam
that drained our energy and patience. These stunted bushes are
tough and wiry, and at times they completely block a climber's
way. I had taken careful note of where we last saw the moose and
we were finally very close to that spot. We proceeded cautiously
upward along the ridge, above a small creek, which provided us
a good view over the islands of balsam still around us. All three
of us saw the moose at once. They were on the move, perhaps

hearing our approach, and disappeared over a small rise. I posted Dave where we were and sent Mike straight to where the moose had just disappeared. I went up higher, hopefully to get a better view.

Mike was no sooner out of my sight when I heard his rifle boom. I hurried back to the sound to find Mike excited. He pointed out where the bull had been; it had run off at the shot. We located a blood spoor immediately and topped a rise to see the bull looking back over his shoulder at us only thirty yards away. Mike fired again and I saw hair fly on the shoulder. The moose collapsed on his hind quarters and did a back flip on the steep slope right onto his head, driving the antlers into the rocks as he went over. As I ran up to the animal, he gave the death rattle and a finishing shot wasn't necessary.

My hunter's excitement was somewhat muted as we approached the animal. That last somersault had completely broken off the right antler and it was only attached by the scalp hide. I told Mike that any taxidermist worth his salt should have no trouble reattaching it.

You won't find nicer country than the alpine slopes high above the timber in the Cassiar Mountains. And here is where we found ourselves one September morning in 1987. "We" were myself and two hunters from Idaho, Dick and Wayne. Dick had killed a fat black bear earlier in the hunt and had killed it with one shot from 200 yards. I called him Dead-Eye Dick for that effort. It was now Wayne's kick at the cat and we were into action.

From down in the valley we saw them, a cow moose and her bull. We climbed for one hour and were now taking a breather as we searched the finger of trees that led up the steep mountain side in front of us. On either side of this 100-yard thick finger it was open with only low brush covering the two sides. Occasionally we could hear cracking sounds from the cover, so we knew the lovers were inside, just out of sight. I was in no hurry to go into the dense cover as the keen-eared moose would hear us for sure. After an hour's wait we slowly worked our way up along side this patch of bush, peering in hopefully to locate the moose. The breeze was coming nicely toward us so I had no fears in that regard. We were high up the mountain now and looking directly down into the finger of forest where the moose were but they were still out of sight and probably bedded down now, as all was quiet. A new tactic was required.

I told Dick to give Wayne and me fifteen minutes to get into position back down in the middle of the open area on the downwind side of the moose. He was then to proceed down the upwind side. My idea was that the moose would smell Dick and I was sure they would flee right toward Wayne and me—we were not disappointed.

Wayne picked out a good shooting position on top of a large boulder and I scanned the edge of the cover. Soon, out stepped a cow moose moving rapidly away from the trees and going straight down the mountain. Where she originally emerged was about 250 yards from us and she was moving farther away with every step. Then the unexpected happened, as it often does with hunting, the cow made a large U-turn and walked back up the open slide toward us. She finally stopped about seventy-five yards below us and looked back expectantly to where she had just come. I whispered to Wayne, "here comes the bull."

Sure enough, the bull emerged exactly where the cow had and Wayne wanted to try the long 250 yard shot. I told him to wait as this big-antlered bull would sniff his way right up to the cow. Wayne looked at me apprehensively as the bull walked down the slope away from us, but he was taking the cow's route exactly and soon was making the big U-turn himself. We let him walk right up to the cow and Wayne fired the second he stopped. I was watching through my binoculars and the bull instantly disappeared and I didn't even see a hit. The cow ran off at the shot, crashing through the low bush as she went.

We stayed put for a few minutes to see if the bull would follow but he was nowhere to be found. I left Wayne on his perch to keep a lookout while I went down to investigate. Down in a low depression lay the huge-bodied moose.

When a beginning hunter sees his quarry lying before him for the first time, the size of a moose is astonishing. Most Americans have only hunted deer and just can't get over the size of our big moose. Dick came stumbling down the hill side to join us and his first words were, "How are we going to get this monster back down to the boat?"

This bull had nice antlers that would measure about forty-eight inches across and they swept up high. I would estimate his live weight to be over 1,500 pounds. We all took photos and then the work began. I carry a small meat saw and, after gutting the bull, I put the two men to work sawing it down to four quarters while I worked on the cape. We had no horses to help on this trip and all the packing would be done the hard way, on our backs. I carried the antlers and cape, a load of about 100 pounds, and the other men each took a hind quarter that would weigh right about 175 pounds apiece. It took two trips to pack out all the meat and it was three dog-tired men who arrived in camp that night, long after dark. Dead-Eyed Dick and One-Shot Wayne both know what the term hard hunting means.

# Learning the Hard Way

I once had a city slicker ask me, "What would happen if you had an accident out here alone on the trapline?" My answer was simple, "I don't have accidents." The old axiom "don't take chances" is law for any man who habitually travels alone in the bush. I learned long ago that it's the small things that can kill a man.

Humans are comfortable at 20°C but at -30°C we are definitely not in our element. I forgot to dry out the felt liners in my boots one night and froze my big toe the next day. Whenever the weather turns cold that toe reminds me of how stupid I was. "Never walk a log" is another lesson I've learned the hard way. It's tempting when traveling in blown down timber country to stay above the mess by walking on the highest log. A slip off is easy when the rotten bark on a slimy wet log gives way under a man's foot. I cracked a couple of ribs doing just this thing one spring day and it hurt to breathe for a month afterwards.

Recreational snowmobilers use the buddy system when traveling over the winter snows in remote country. By contrast, the trapper always works alone. I carry tools and spare parts for my Tundra snowmobile, but sometimes the machine still leaves me stranded. In the old days when a trapper only used his two feet he was never more than a day's walk from the cabin. A snowmobile can leave a man miles from shelter in a very short time.

My snowmobile had completely died and I was walking to my cabin only two miles away. I had an hour of daylight left, my backpack was not too heavy and my snowshoes made walking easy. I soon reached my little shack on the Salmon River and in no time had the fire going and supper in the frying pan.

Morning came and I opened a can of corned beef to fry up with my pancakes. This was one of those cans that use a key to open the seam. I had forgotten to put this can in the hole in the ground where I put other canned goods to keep them from freezing. The canned meat had frozen and thawed a few times and I guess the can had split open at the seam. The meat seemed to smell all right and I ate the whole works along with a few pancakes.

It was about eight miles out to my truck, parked on the nearest logging road, but the going was tough due to a fresh fall of snow during the night. I started out full of breakfast and energy. Eight miles by snowshoe is no problem for a healthy man. I was carrying about forty pounds of frozen marten, bait meat, traps, ax and rifle on my Trapper Nelson packboard. About an hour into my journey I began to get sick to my stomach. A short while later, I began to sweat profusely and my legs began to get tired. By noon, I was sick as a dog and so weak I'd have to lean against a tree to cuss.

I knew it was going to be a long night if I had to bivouac out under the spruce trees in my condition. By then I was an equal distance from the cabin or the truck. I cached my traps, marten and other gear to lessen my load, keeping only my ax and a little dried moose jerky with me. I was determined to make the truck and drive the thirty miles to home and comfort. Well, that last four miles was the longest in my life. I would walk 100 yards and rest. Each time I sat down, it was harder to get up again. A four or five-hour trip in the end turned into an eight-hour torture test. That old Dodge pickup was a welcome sight. Lesson learned— throw out any canned goods that have frozen.

Thunk, thunk, my ax swinging with every other step, I checked the thickness of the river ice under my feet. A good hard swing will produce a different sound between thick and thin ice. If the ax hole gets wet with water, back off. The weather had been cold for a week and even the rapids were frozen over on the Salmon River. The temperature was about -25°C as I made my way up river. I had my usual thirty-pound pack on my back and was carrying my snowshoes under my arm. If a man goes through the ice with his snowshoes on, he's in trouble because with every kick he pulls himself deeper.

I was heading for my sure-fire mink trap at the point where a small creek enters the main river. Mink like to travel these routes and I'd already caught a big male here the week before. The ice is always dangerous around beaver lodges, dams and especially those entering creeks. My trap was four feet above the river level on a clay bank and the ice seemed safe. I was in the process of removing a white weasel (ermine) from the trap when the ice cracked under my feet. Before I could jump for the bank, the ice broke and I fell into waist deep water. I clawed my way up the bank by grabbing the willow bushes, not an easy feat with my backpack and heavy, wet wool clothes. Luckily, I had set my snowshoes up on the bank when I first arrived. When I was clear of the water and safely up on shore I shucked my pack, lay down and rolled around on the powdery snow. The snow acted as a blotter to soak up a lot of the water from my pants.

I now had two choices, make for the timber to get a fire going or head for my cabin only a mile away. I chose the latter. My pants instantly froze solid like stovepipes, but the two pairs of long johns I wore underneath were still keeping my legs from freezing. I strapped on the snowshoes and, leaving the backpack behind, made a beeline for the cabin. My feet were two blocks of ice by the time that log shack came into sight. My fire from the night before still showed signs of life and I quickly stoked it up.

153

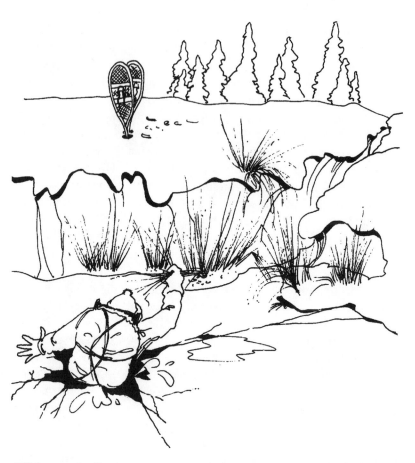

With numb fingers I had a difficult time getting my frozen clothes peeled off and had to cut the top laces on my boots. It wasn't long, however, before that old wood heater had me all thawed out and back to normal.

The river was swollen, brown and ugly at the height of the spring runoff. My brother Pat and I were taking advantage of the high water to move supplies up river to a trap cabin I was building. My old wooden riverboat was loaded down heavily with plywood, lumber, roofing tin and numerous other supplies.

Long sweepers (fallen trees) lay in the river and these were catching trees that were being swept downstream by the high water. As I piloted the old boat against the current I had to steer around these obstacles every so often. Around one bend we discovered the river blocked off by a high spruce tree that had fallen and had hooked its top on the opposite shore. Several logs and assorted debris had begun to pile against this tree and it was badly bowed with these and the force of the current. I eased the nose of the boat up to the center of the log and held it there with the kicker. Pat fired up the chainsaw and began to saw the tree, water flying up behind him, as the blade was under the surface. He had just started when the tree broke with a mighty crack. I guess I must have had the bow partially resting on the tree itself because one half of it caught the bow and swung us instantly to shore pinning us to the bank. The logs and debris that were now released scraped the trapped boat as they rushed downstream past us. I was frantically trying to push these off with my pole, but one big log punched a hole in the side near the stern and water rushed in through the twelve-inch gash. "Throw all the gear on shore!" I hollered at Pat and you never saw two men empty a boat so fast in your life. I tied a stern line fast to a spruce tree so the stern and motor would not go under, as the boat was filling with water at a terrific rate.

Two hours later we had patched up the boat, loaded up the freight and were again on our way.

# Secrets of the Deep

The campfire was burning, throwing spruce sparks high into the night air and making the shadows dance on the encircling trees. This is the time to reminisce about old hunts, favorite rifles and dogs and strange unsolved mysteries of the bush.

Each of the hundreds of lakes in the interior of B.C. has a history of its own. The names given to many of these lakes all have stories behind them. Hoodoo Lake got its unusual name from the early surveyors.

Just after the turn of the century, a pack train of supplies was being unloaded from the horses onto a log raft at the east end of lower Hoodoo Lake. The surveyors then poled and paddled their way across to the other side. Once there, they split up to mark and survey this new country. When night fell, one man didn't show up. The search began at dawn and it was noon before the lost man was found. The party, now reunited, again set off for the upper lake in the raft. A wind arose and, before the ungainly craft could be paddled to shore, it capsized. The men lost all their gear, including their expensive transit, to the bottom where it still lies to this day. The men saved themselves but had to walk the thirty miles back to the Indian settlement of Fort George. A few weeks later the surveyors returned to complete their work. While setting up camp near shore one man cut himself badly with an axe. The injured man had to be carried back to civilization and the surveying task was now postponed until the following summer. This was definitely a bad luck lake, it was jinxed or hoodooed—hence Hoodoo Lake became its name.

When old timers meet and the name Chief Lake is mentioned, an uneasiness often comes over the group. Looking at this five-mile long lake on a calm day, a newcomer sees only a picturesque lake surrounded by low hills. This body of water, however, has seen its share of tragedy and mystery.

I've mentioned elsewhere in this book how a trapper named Clayton lost his life in the dark waters of Chief Lake. Only a little while later the man that moved into Clayton's cabin also drowned in the lake.

Chief Lake was named for the Carrier Indian tribes that met along its shore every spring after the winter's trapping season. These early Indians undoubtedly had stories of their own to tell about the treacherous ice conditions they encountered on Chief Lake. As early as 1920 the first white trapper drowned in its waters. In the early 1930s two more trappers lost their lives there, including a well-known bush man named Winka. About this time a horseman was thrown from the saddle and kicked to death when his horse slipped on the ice.

In the 1930s several homesteaders cut ties for the railroad around the well-treed shoreline of Chief Lake. My neighbor and old-time trapper Bert Peterson related to me how he nearly became another one of Chief Lake's tragic statistics. Bert and another man had cut and hewn several hundred ties in the winter of 1938/39. Early spring found them loading up their truck with these ties to take them out to Prince George. They loaded only sixty ties on that first trip and made it across the lake icewithout any problems. The next trip they loaded eighty ties and again got across safely. The third trip was trouble—this time the truck was loaded with 100 ties and part way across the lake, the back wheels broke through. Both men instantly bailed out of the cab as the truck began to slip backwards into the hole. Fortunately, the truck stuck and, with help from others, the rig was pulled out, minus its load. By now the truck owner had had enough of Chief Lake.

Never one to say die, Bert and his partner now enlisted another man with a team of horses and sleigh to haul their ties across for them. The sleigh was loaded up and the four horses started across. The teamster told Bert to ride behind the horses just in front of the loaded sleigh; that way he could pull the main pin to free the horses if anything happened. Chief Lake has little patience with men who tempt it. Sure enough the loaded sleigh broke through and Bert couldn't budge the pin to free the horses. Things were serious but luck was with the men again as the load of ties bound to the sled hung up on the ice. The team didn't panic and Bert finally got the pin pulled. The men learned their lesson and the ties were finally barged across when open water came that spring.

In 1967 another mystery occurred at Chief Lake. When the ice melted that spring, a body was found. An accident? Maybe, but this corpse had an iron weight tied to its neck.

For many years there was a general store and post office at the east end of Chief Lake. The store owner was a man named Ferguson. One cold night in 1957 the winter sky was lit up for miles around. The store had caught on fire and Mr. Ferguson was not able to escape. The man lived alone in the back of the store and the authorities couldn't understand why he had not made it out when the fire started. Add yet another mystery to the many that occurred at Chief Lake.

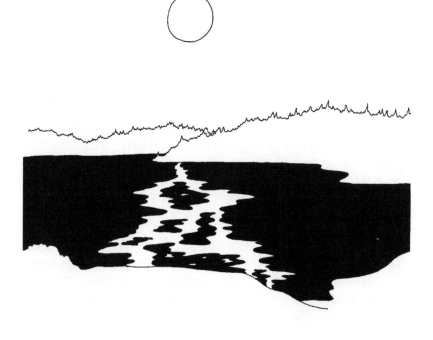

# Only the Strong Survive

Brotherly love is a rare commodity in the wilderness. A wild animal's first and only priority is to look out for Number One. I know this sounds overly harsh but it's cold reality. There is considerable affection between mother and young but this affection nearly always disappears as the young grow up. The moose is a good example of a strong bond between cow and calf, but in the spring of the year a ritual takes place that I've seen on numerous occasions.

The yearling calf, almost fully grown, was on one side of the small river and the cow moose was on the other side. The cow had her hair raised and ears laid back. The youngster was confused and again ran across through the shallow water to join his mom with whom he'd just spent the first year of his life. The same mother who had helped him through the snow drifts and protected him from wolves all winter. Before he reached shore the cow attacked him again, biting him and striking out with her front hooves. The calf stumbled to his knees trying to get away from this onslaught. He ran back to the safety of the far bank, the cow at his rump biting him all the way. He frantically ran up into the willows and the cow walked back over to her side. The calf was definitely *persona non grata* as far as the cow moose was concerned. She would soon be dropping this spring's new calf and had no use for her older sibling. The calf henceforth would be a solitary roamer for most of the rest of his life. He would have to protect himself or die.

This past spring I've watched a crippled coyote on a carcass. His hind leg had been damaged and he would have a very difficult time catching anything at his present running speed. The two coyotes already on the kill were not letting the handicapped one have a chance to eat. They would drive him off when he came too close and his lot was to wait patiently out on the lake ice for what would be left. This animal was lucky, however, for if he was a wolf he probably already would be dead.

The wolf has a highly developed instinct to sense weakness and quickly moves in for the kill. A lot of nonsense has been written on how the wolf pack only takes the old and the sick of the moose population. This should read the young and vulnerable. I've never actually seen a sick moose in the wild and even the many old moose I've shot all appeared healthy and strong. The wolf, as I mentioned earlier, kills mostly the young moose calves, as they are the weakest and this apparent weakness triggers the wolf to attack. Even the wolf itself is in danger from this instinct.

A hunter and friend of mine once shot at a wolf that was running across the lake ice; the wolf was with a small pack of six others. The shot was poorly aimed and only succeeded in breaking the wolf's hind leg. The wounded animal yelped and spun around to bite his wounded leg. The rest of the pack, likely some of which were his parents and siblings, turned and attacked the unfortunate beast *en masse*. The hunter, in his excitement, missed all the wolves with his next shot but it was enough to scatter the pack. The wounded animal was near death from the vicious mauling he had just received from his buddies and just lay on the ice as the hunter approached. A finishing shot was not necessary. These wolves had sensed weakness and their automatic pilots kicked in; they couldn't help themselves as the killing instinct was too great to prevent them from attacking their own.

I would caution the reader to not judge nature's ways too harshly. The wild animals do not have the reasoning power that man has, that ability to chose right from wrong. Nature always has its reasons for instilling these behavior instincts in her wild creatures. Whether we agree with them or not, they seem to work for each species.

# Trapline Notes

## Beaver

The beaver is our most important fur bearer in interior British Columbia. Oh, the pine marten is worth more money per animal, as are several other animals, but the quantity of beavers and the ability of the trapper to "farm" them make it the mainstay of the trapline. Even when beaver prices are low, many beavers are trapped each fall as the long-line trapper needs the beaver meat to bait his traps.

The live lodges (beaver houses made of sticks and mud) are easy to locate around the lake shore. By limiting his annual take to two or three animals per house, the trapper ensures a good steady population from year to year. The beaver's main enemies are the wolf and man. The cunning wolf waits until dark when the big rodent is well back in the bush cutting down trees to eat. The wolf then cuts the beaver off from the water and safety and it's the end of "old chisel tooth." The beaver is not a pushover, however, and any canine should be careful when taking him on.

My old buddy Ernie Hall, who lives near our place at Hoodoo Lake, owns a big labrador dog named Spunky. One day Spunky thought he might have a little fun at a beaver's expense and got a rude awakening. The lab caught an old beaver out on a wet marsh but came out second best in the battle. A full-grown beaver weighs fifty pounds or more and this one tore a gash in the dog's lower flank about four inches long. I helped Ernie stitch up his pet and old Spunky is not so brave around beavers anymore.

Coyotes love beaver meat but only rarely get a chance to taste it. I'm sure two or three coyotes working together could kill an adult beaver but one-on-one the beaver would have more than a sporting chance. The coyote is an opportunist. I caught a nice big male beaver at the spillway of a dam on a small lake this winter. I usually leave enough wire on the killing-type trap I use so the animal is able, in his death throes, to reach deep water. This time my trap got hung up on a stick and the beaver died partially out of the water. As I approached the set I could see coyote tracks on the snow-covered lake ice. Sure enough, two coyotes had half-eaten my beaver ruining a $40 pelt.

## Porcupine

This prickly fellow is not a fur bearer but I see him often in my travels in the bush. For the most part, I leave this slow animal alone, but I've had to kill the odd one around my cabins and boats. They chew anything with salt or glue in it. A plywood boat or outhouse is soon ruined if porcupines are around.

I've never eaten the porcupine but I've heard from others that it's not bad table fare. The Indians used to throw the entire animal into the fire to burn off the quills first. The quills are used to decorate various garments and the hunters I guide like to put a few in their hat bands. I once told a hunter that if we saw a porky he could get a few quills by slapping his hat against the animal. It wasn't long before we spied one crossing a logging road, so my hunter leaped out of the truck and chased the porcupine down. Instead of slapping the animal with his hat, he threw it at the porky from close range and his Stetson stuck! I was breaking up with laughter watching that man chasing the porcupine around trying to get his new hat back.

One late spring day, about June 10, I witnessed an unusual sight. We've all heard jokes about how porcupines mate—carefully. I was sitting outside my cabin at the meeting of the Muskeg and Salmon Rivers enjoying the warm sunshine when two porcupines lumbered out of the willows into the open. The larger one was chasing the smaller one and they began to rough and tumble just like two friendly dogs. I'm sure the larger male was attempting to mate with the female as he kept trying to roll her over. She wasn't ready, I guess, because she would give him a light slap with her tail in the face. The male would then vigorously rub his face with his front paws to remove the quills and then the courting would continue. I watched the two animals for more than

thirty minutes and finally the female lay on her back so the male could mount her.

## Weasel

This little animal is the smallest carnivore, apart from the shrew. A prime white weasel, or ermine as the furriers call it, is worth about nine dollars to the trapper. When the mice are thick, the weasel is abundant as they are real mousers. The weasel also kills squirrels by going right down the holes into the cone pile nests that the squirrels make. Many weasels are caught incidentally in the traps set for marten. They are fearless, bold little fellows and I've had them come right up to my feet when I was sitting quietly on a log. Once an American hunter and I pitched our three man pup tent high above timberline near Tatlatui Park in northern B.C. I had just finished erecting the tent and was rustling up some grub for supper when the tent came alive! A curious brown weasel had gotten inside and the wind blew the tent flap shut. That weasel was hitting the inside of the tent up and down and back and forth, frantic to get out.

I was sleeping one fall in one of my little line cabins and, as usual, the mice were not in short supply. As soon as I put out the candle and was quiet, the mice began to hold a track meet on the floor around me. Around midnight the action really picked up with mice scurrying everywhere and I could even hear them squeaking. At one point the salt shaker fell over on the table so I knew there had to be something bigger than a mouse inside. I reached under my bunk where I kept my flashlight and trained it on the table. There, looking back at me, was a large male weasel with a mouse in its mouth. I switched off the light and never heard a mouse the rest of the night.

## Flying Squirrels

I've only seen four or five flying squirrels alive in my life yet there are literally thousands on my trapline. The reason for this is that these little mammals are nocturnal—they only come out at night. Each winter I catch many in my marten and mink trap sets. I'm not trying to trap them, as there is no market for their pelts, and I wish I could discover a way to keep them out of the traps.

They are definitely fond of beaver meat as that is what I bait my trap stations with. I don't know what they normally eat when they fly about at night. Of course, they don't actually fly, but just glide from tree to tree. I have one cabin where it's a rare evening that I don't hear one of these night flyers land with a thump on the tin roof and run across before jumping off.

The flying squirrel has strange glassy eyes that he uses to see in the dark. He has a flap of loose skin that runs the entire length of his body on both sides. He opens this flap up when he leaps off a tree and I once saw one glide about 100 feet out from the tree and land on the ground.

## Coyotes

Coyotes are survivors. The wolf needs large tracts of wilderness to exist. The wild fox almost needs man and his agriculture to do well because in truly wild country he barely ekes out a living and is easy pickings for both wolf and coyote when the snows are deep. The coyote does well in all kinds of situations. He is equally at home in rural farm land, open prairie, or the wildest forest land. He is usually too quick for the wolf to eat and his only enemy besides man is disease, particularly mange.

I remember in my early years of trapping, when I thought I knew everything and actually knew nothing, wondering why I could not catch coyotes in my lynx cubbies and other sets. The coyote is a smart customer. The fox has a reputation for being clever but the coyote is head and shoulders above his lesser cousin when it comes to using his brain. I've had coyotes walk up to a cleverly placed snare wire, sniff it and walk around with impunity. The real expert trappers use the dirt hole trap set in early winter to catch their quota of coyotes.

I enjoy watching the coyote and have seen him spend hours catching mice in the fields. He is a scavenger and I shoot many each year over bait piles, usually cattle carcasses I set out on my trapline. The coyotes' pelt is prime in late November and by February I leave him alone as by then his fur is below par. Each spring I drag a carcass out in front of my home on Hoodoo Lake to feed the bald eagles, coyotes and foxes. My family and I enjoy watching these animals throughout the late winter months. Last

March we observed five coyotes at one time, feeding. There is always a pecking order and the boss coyote drives the others away until he is fed. The bald eagles wait patiently for the coyotes to finish and then it's their turn. This spring I witnessed an unusual sight. A big eagle was on the dead steer when a lone coyote approached. The coyote walked up to drive the eagle off but the eagle had different ideas. The bird fanned out its wings and, with his talons stretched out in front of him, came at the coyote. The coyote was thoroughly intimidated and withdrew to wait for his turn later.

The coyote is an opportunist. One early summer day a few years ago I was giving the cow boss on the Bar K Ranch (located twenty miles north of Prince George) a hand checking over the herd. It was a warm day in June and Rod and I were riding a couple of spirited horses. Rod was the real cowboy and did any roping that was required. We would approach the cows with their young calves and check the little ones for scours or hoof trouble. Rod roped several that morning and I helped him administer antibiotic inoculations. The ranch had lost a few calves to wolves, coyotes and even eagles. The eagles actually didn't kill the calves but only blinded them by pecking out their eyes when they were first born.

Rod asked me to check out a group of cows with newborn calves that were about 200 yards from the timber. As I rode up, I noticed a coyote slinking over in the tall grass toward a little Hereford calf. The mother cow had left the sleeping calf and was grazing some distance off. The coyote was so intent on his prey he didn't notice my approach. I was riding a fast three-year-old filly named Foxy. The coyote finally saw me and bolted for the timber just as I spurred the horse. We raced flat out but the coyote was no match for that horse. If I had been any good with a rope I could easily have lassoed that "doggie." I finally reined in Foxy and let the frantic coyote go his way. It will be a while before that coyote has enough nerve to go after cattle again.

## Birds

The ravens hang around throughout the winter. They don't migrate south as the crows do, but prefer to tough out the weather.

When the smaller crows arrive back in March, they drive away the slower-flying ravens. The crows also give the great horned owl a hard time if the owl happens to get caught out during the daylight hours. This hatred for owls is completely understandable because when night comes the tables are turned. Nightfall is a time of danger for many animals and the great horned owl is often the villain. This owl glides quietly through the dark forest and, using his powerful talons, catches not only the snowshoe hare and flying squirrel but also knocks off from their perch grouse and especially crows. These latter two birds have no night vision and can only sit in terror as the owl swoops down on them. No wonder the crow is out for revenge during the day.

Time was definitely not on the swan's side. November 25 and all the lakes had frozen over two weeks earlier. The river was freezing, too, at least in all the slower sections. The big bird had been in the open spot for some time as I could see where he had been climbing out onto the snow-covered shore in many places. I threw a snowball at him as I walked along the shore. A healthy swan would have flown off as I was too close for this normally timid animal to tolerate, but this bird only swam away to the far bank. I surmised that, for whatever reason, the swan couldn't fly or he would be with others of his kind down south or at least over on the Crooked River where open water exists all winter.

Three days later I was returning past the spot after checking my trapline up river and, sure enough, my unseasonable guest was still in his shrinking spot of open water at the foot of the rapids. It was getting colder every day and the steam was rising from the water. This last open spot would soon be frozen over. I wished the swan good luck as it would be several days before I would be back this way.

The temperature was about -25°C as I rode my skidoo down to the line cabin on the Salmon River this early December morning. I put on my snowshoes and set out up river. When I came to the swan's resting place, the river was now completely frozen over with no sign of the bird. I did notice fresh tracks around the river's bank though—the tracks of a fox.

# In Retrospect

A buddy and I once watched a small lake freeze over and then thaw out in the warm afternoon sun. We did this over a twelve-hour period. We were waiting patiently for a float plane to pick us up after a seven-day wilderness trip. That was about as close as I have ever come to being bored. It seems there is always something to do in the bush. I have always enjoyed my work because it never seemed like work.

The twenty-four years I have lived in the north have gone by quickly. At forty-eight years of age I'm in excellent health and am looking forward to adventures that lie ahead.

This summer (1996) we are taking a riverboat trip down the Lower Stikine River to Wrangell, Alaska. I've heard there are more than twenty glaciers visible from the river and the fishing should be excellent.

I've just completed a successful spring hunt with an American, for black bear. This was his first with a bow and arrow. I can still see the excitement flashing in his eyes as we stalked so close to the bear that we could hear him chewing on clover.

Writing this book has been very enjoyable for me as I was able to relive a lot of good times. It has been gratifying to see my children, especially my three sons, grow up with an appreciation of the wild country. My hope is that you, the reader, not only enjoy my stories but also gain in your love of our beautiful wild country.

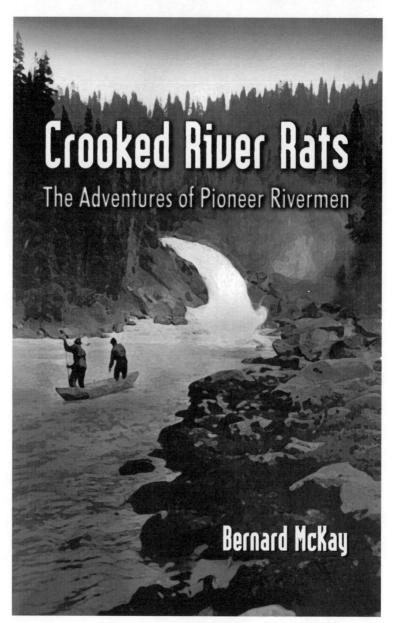

# Crooked River Rats
## The Adventures of Pioneer Rivermen

### Bernard McKay

**Bernard McKay**
**5 1/2 x 8 1/2, 176 pp., SC    ISBN 0-88839-451-9**

*New!* Also available from HANCOCK HOUSE

# YUKON
# RIVERBOAT
# DAYS

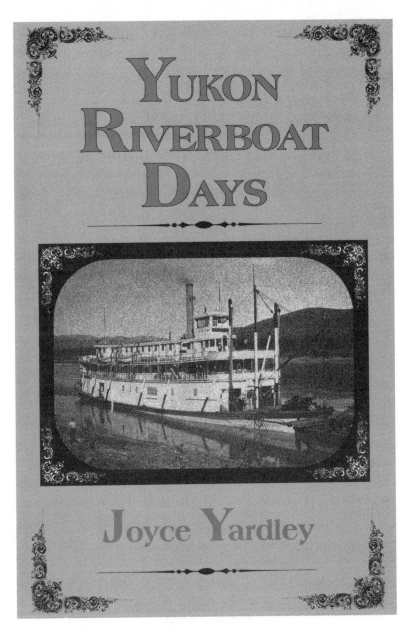

## Joyce Yardley

**Joyce Yardley**
**5 1/2 x 8 1/2, 192 pp., SC   ISBN 0-88839-386-5**

Available from Hancock House Publishers, 19313 Zero Ave., Surrey, B.C. V4P 1M7
1-800-938-1114  Fax (604) 538-2262       1431 Harrison Ave., Blaine, WA 98230

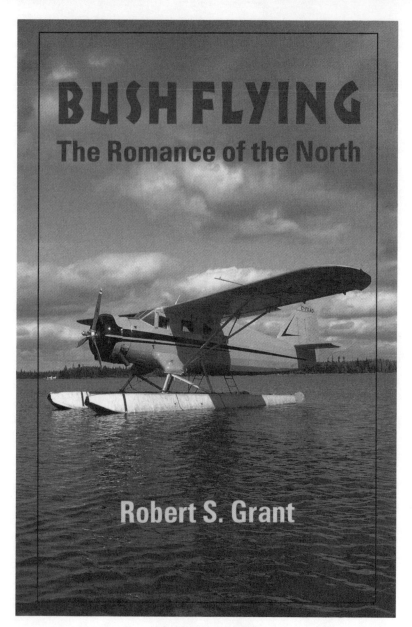

# BUSH FLYING
## The Romance of the North

### Robert S. Grant

**Robert S. Grant**
**5 1/2 x 8 1/2, 288 pp., SC   ISBN 0-88839-350-4**

Available from Hancock House Publishers, 19313 Zero Ave., Surrey, B.C. V4P 1M7
1-800-938-1114  Fax (604) 538-2262      1431 Harrison Ave., Blaine, WA 98230

# Still Rhymin' on the Range

**Mike Puhallo, Brian Brannon, Wendy Liddle**
**5 1/2 x 8 1/2, 64 pp., SC   ISBN 0-88839-388-1**

Available from Hancock House Publishers, 19313 Zero Ave., Surrey, B.C. V4P 1M7
1-800-938-1114  Fax (604) 538-2262        1431 Harrison Ave., Blaine, WA 98230

## *History*

**Barkerville**
Lorraine Harris
ISBN 0-88839-152-8

**Border Heritage**
Jens Skolleborg
ISBN 0-88839-275-5

**B.C.'s Own Railroad**
Lorraine Harris
ISBN 0-88839-125-0

**Cariboo Gold Rush Story**
Donald Waite
ISBN 0-88839-202-8

**The Craigmont Story**
Murphy Shewchuck
ISBN 0-88839-980-4

**Curse of Gold**
Elizabeth Hawkins
ISBN 0-88839-281-8

**Early History of Port Moody**
Dorathea M. Norton
ISBN 0-88839-197-8

**End of Custer**
Dale T. Schoenberger
ISBN 0-88839-288-5

**Exploring the Outdoors**
Eberts & Grass
ISBN 0-88839-989-8

**Fraser Canyon Highway**
Lorraine Harris
ISBN 0-88839-182-X

**Fraser Canyon Story**
Donald E. Waite
ISBN 0-88839-204-4

**Fraser Valley Story**
Donald E. Waite
ISBN0-88839-203-6

**Guide to Gold Panning**
Bill Barlee
ISBN 0-88839-986-3

**Guide to Similkameen Treasure**
Bill Barlee
ISBN 0-88839-990-1

**Gold Creeks & Ghost Towns**
Bill Barlee
ISBN 0-88839-988-X

**Gold! Gold!**
Joseph Petralia
ISBN 0-88839-118-8

**Living with Logs**
Donovan Clemson
ISBN 0-919654-10-X

**Logging in B.C.**
Ed Gould
ISBN 0-919654-44-4

**Lost Mines and Historic Treasures**
Bill Barlee
ISBN 0-88839-992-8

**The Mackenzie Yesterday**
Alfred Aquilina
ISBN 0-88839-083-1

**Old Wooden Buildings**
Donovan Clemson
ISBN 0-919654-90-8

**Pacific Northwest History**
Edward Nuffield
ISBN 0-88839-271-0

# MORE GREAT HANCOCK HOUSE TITLES

**Pioneering Aviation of the West**
Lloyd M. Bungey
ISBN 0-88839-271-0

**Yukon Places & Names**
R. Coutts
ISBN 0-88839-082-2

## Northern Biographies

**Alaska Calls**
Virginia Neely
ISBN 0-88839-970-7

**Bootlegger's Lady**
Sager & Frye
ISBN 0-88839-976-6

**Bush Flying**
Robert Grant
ISBN 0-88839-350-4

**Crazy Cooks and Gold Miners**
Joyce Yardley
ISBN 0-88839-294-X

**Descent into Madness**
Vernon Frolick
ISBN 0-88839-300-8

**Fogswamp: Life with Swans**
Turner & McVeigh
ISBN 0-88839-104-8

**Gang Ranch: Real Story**
Judy Alsager
ISBN 0-88839-275-3

**Journal of Country Lawyer**
Ted Burton
ISBN 0-88839-364-4

**Lady Rancher**
Gertrude Roger
ISBN 0-88839-099-8

**Nahanni**
Dick Turner
ISBN 0-88839-028-9

**Northern Man**
Jim Martin
ISBN 0-88839-979-0

**Novice in the North**
Bill Robinson
ISBN 0-88839-977-4

**Puffin Cove**
Neil G. Carey
ISBN 0-88839-216-8

**Ralph Edwards of Lonesome Lake**
Ed Gould
ISBN 0-88839-100-5

**Ruffles on my Longjohns**
Isabel Edwards
ISBN 0-88839-102-1

**Where Mountains Touch Heaven**
Ena Kingsnorth Powell
ISBN 0-88839-365-2

**Wings of the North**
Dick Turner
ISBN 0-88839-060-2

**Yukon Lady**
Hugh McLean
ISBN 0-88839-186-2

**Yukoners**
Harry Gordon-Cooper
ISBN 0-88839-232-X